Dead Reckoning

Paul McMahon

For Molly

~ 3 ~

Paul McMahon – Dead Reckoning

This is a work of fiction.

"In the midst of this chopping sea of civilized life, such are the clouds and storms and quicksands and thousand-and-one items to be allowed for, that a man has to live, if he would not founder and go to the bottom and not make his port at all, by dead reckoning, and he must be a great calculator indeed who succeeds."

Henry David Thoreau 1849

Walden

…I have no idea what happened up to this point either.

Right now, I can recall nothing; relevant or otherwise about last night's events, apart from being excessively polite to some energetic policeman, prior to some pain. As an amnesia veteran I realise the importance of establishing the facts pre-panic, so I pry open one solitary eye to investigate. I am immediately bedazzled by bulb-light and ill focus which upsets my body's delicate harmony and I have to resist the urge to purge. I am momentarily fixated on the blood banging boisterously in my head, when an uncharted voice suddenly screams at me:

Voice: MORNING!

This catches me completely unawares and powerless to prevent my body's instinctual reaction to fling open wide my remaining eye, flooding my vision and basking me in headache.

(1)**Pragmatic competence:**

I am fully aware I don't really have the time to contemplate it right now, but the thought insolently occurs to me anyway, that an entire linguistic subfield should be dedicated to this mystery maestro of brevity. With one single utterance, he has masterfully managed to one-word-whip me into a duo-layered comprehension that -

1. It is definitely **not** morning.

2. I have without doubt committed a monumental faux pas.

Paul McMahon – Dead Reckoning

My work has made me immensely sensitive to implicature, and his sarcasm is so heavy I could moor a yacht to it.

There is a that sounds like it has been left for me to apologise. However, not knowing what I have done, and therefore unaware which words are appropriate to wrap either side of "...sorry...", I elect to play it safe and wait for another clue in order to contextualise my imminent apology. Eyeing my dazed bewilderment and sensing my memory's reluctance to participate in my own degradation, this blurry black and white shape offers to fill in all the blanks for me.

Do not pass go, do not collect £200

Apparently his unit arrived on scene at a residential address in Balham, in response to a call from a couple of very bemused elderly homeowners, and had reason to apprehend a man, with a description not dissimilar to mine, as he was trying to gain access to the front door of this aforementioned residential address. The shape goes onto explain that when challenged, the suspect dismissed the Police Constables, asserting "...there is nothing to see here Ossifers, go about your business". Upon further investigation at the scene, the suspect insisted that he lived at the address, which was in fact a vessel. Moreover, when the owners opened the door to thank the police for their swift response, the suspect demanded that the officers arrest the OAPs for 'mutiny'. This allegation was dismissed, much to the annoyance of the suspect who insisted on being correctly addressed at this juncture as "Captain". The perpetrator apparently couldn't understand why his key didn't fit the front door and was scream-slurring at the male occupant, snarling "locksmith" like it were an expletive.

Paul McMahon – Dead Reckoning

Look one way and row another

Having never lived In Balham I can offer no explanation to the sergeant for my being there. I simply apologise profusely and say something random about a non-existent stag do. It appears that he has thoroughly enjoyed every moment of my mortification, and his delight looks to be my saving grace. With a polished boot he slides a yellow hazard bag across the floor to me containing –

1 x pair of black uniform trousers

1 x white shirt I recognise

He tosses a small evidence bag, which contains the rest of my possessions, onto the blue plastic mattress I am swaying upon. He does all this whilst wiping a tear out of the corner of his eye. I begin to sense the end of my humiliation is nigh when up pops a WPC with a bucket and a pair of yellow marigolds which she holds outstretched to me. A few sexist gags cross my mind which I am able to suppress, leaving me with nothing. I am at a loss. The sight is too surreal and out of context for me to have a stab at decoding, especially with a hangover the size of the pacific. My flummoxedness must be written all over my face, as she smiles smugly and helpfully points at the wall behind my head.

Penny drops:

Now. Albeit the Large Brown Capitals *look* like my writing, the letters spell out *my* full name, and the damp sensation around my back end may all very well be connected, I still stand to investigate, desperately hoping to find an alternative explanation to the one suddenly assaulting my nostrils, only to find this new altitude has an adverse effect on my gag reflex. I battle for balance and in doing so centre my gaze on the floor below me, in the foreground of which I see about my ankles, a soiled all in one, white, paper jump suit, and thus my nickname is borne.

A fish out of water:

I know full well that this police station's custody area is going to be full of scumbags picked up during last night's post-pub trawl, and I am desperate to give them all a wide berth in case I recognise any of them or, more precisely, they recognise me. My shame must be evident through my body language, or it might have been my plea for discretion that's given them the idea as, in what can only be a tactic to teach me a damn good lesson, I am deliberately steered toward the front custody desk under the shabby pretext of some administrative necessity or another, for one final humiliation.

The Sergeant makes it *very* clear that I am being done a *favour* getting let off with a slap on the wrist for 'drunk and disorderly'. Apparently my attempt to resist arrest was so pathetic that it doesn't really warrant being recorded, and the arresting offer reportedly found my drunk and incoherent attempts at abuse so funny he has already tagged his own locker with 'landlubber'. All in all I am told, I am a very lucky boy.

Through the fingers of my right hand, that I'm holding up to mask my face from detection, I can see several low-lifes, sat on plastic chairs further down the custody suite, at various stages of liberty-stripping. There is a tense atmosphere and somewhere out of sight, I can hear one man losing an argument about providing a breath sample. An agitated voice suddenly shouts "Officer" and I almost turn round - this would give the game away in a heartbeat. I edge a dangerous little gander over my shoulder and see there is a sleeping tramp sat directly behind me whom I definitely know; I remember making my acquaintance with him only last week at work while I was at the dry end of a fire hose, cleaning him off with the wet end upon his reception into prison. As I recall he didn't appreciate it as much as we did. I remember him distinctly as he's Dutch, and I find accents very amusing. It's highly likely he is on his way back to Prison, and my one services this police station; I am desperate to get out of this shit hole before he wakes up.

There are two Uniform Police Officers behind the desk that I should probably recognise, seeing as they are sniggering and shooting knowing looks over to me where I am groggily swaying sea sick from foot to foot. One of these comic-coppers asks me extremely LOUDLY how it feels to have been banged up for a change. I tortoise my neck in as far as I can, as his decibel level is well within tramp waking range. This 'Loudmouth' is clearly not respecting my obvious attempt to blend in unnoticed. If this episode is teaching me anything, it is that my instinctual desire to call him a *fucking cunt* would probably breach public order section 5, and give Loudmouth more ammunition to publicly hang me out to dry, so I bite my tongue and avert my gaze.

My newly averted gaze happily lands upon a woman stood further down the desk to where I am, dressed in an extremely tight and very short red dress which is exposing the bottom of her bottom. She is leaning disinterested up against the desk looking bored as her charges are read out, presumably trying to take the weight off her enormous heels. Her particular errors of judgement are 'possession of a class A' and 'soliciting' apparently, which I bet she is exceptionally good at. She is standing side on, and from this angle I can see the contours of her incredible body. Even though I can't see her face, through her long hair, I think I would be hard pushed to say no - price permitting. I am de-distracted from this diversion by the other comic copper who makes a literary joke about the 'taming of the screw'. They really are loving this, and I have to admit that one was pretty clever; I can see what he's done there with a play on the prison officer slang. Awkwardly, so might anyone else who may have been listening. What a Wanker.

To fish in troubled waters:

It becomes clear to me that I have the hangover horn, as I am now mesmerized by 'Tight dress' further down the desk. I can see that this is an absurd set of circumstances in which to try and pull, but nonetheless it is becoming obvious to me that my ego is going to have a crack. I am becoming preoccupied with making eye contact with her, so much so that I am unable to give my freedom the attention it so urgently deserves. This is largely in part due to her fantastically distracting body, and I find myself flicking her another look - just in time to see her turn her potentially gorgeous 'boat-race' away from me. The Sergeant reclaims my attention by reading my address to me out loudly. I say yes, even though I haven't really been listening and don't know if this was a question or even my queue to speak. I snatch another quick peek over at Tight dress in time to see that something has finally captured her interest, although I have missed whatever it is, as she is now scribbling something down on a piece of paper. The Sergeants 'excuse-me cough' interrupts my perve, and when I look back he thrusts a form at me across the desk with a disapproving eyebrow. I pick up a biro on one of those little annoying chains which doesn't quite reach the form, despite me frustratedly tugging it twice. I am so tired and confused I feel like an anchovy with an abacus. The Sergeant breaks his attention away from his own form filling - long enough to tut, shake his head, and slide my form an inch toward the immovable pen before returning to his jottings. I quickly glance over toward Tight dress to check she didn't witness my moment of stupidity and am relieved to see that she is pre-occupied, folding something up and tucking it into her lucky red bra.

Plenty more (healthy) fish in the sea:

Inconveniently, it seems my embarrassment is almost over. I am walked past the sleeping Dutch tramp, who I now suspect might actually be deceased, toward the security doors which lead to reception by the less annoying one of the comic-coppers, the one with the literary sense of humour. In a last ditch effort to attract her attention I cough melodramatically loudly, but 'Tight dress' doesn't turn around. She doesn't even turn around when I accidently-on-purpose kick over a bin on the way to the doors, which immediately disproves my dead tramp theory as he springs off his chair onto the floor, screaming:

Tramp: Inshcomiiiiiiiiiing!

Everybody in the custody suite looks round at the flying Dutchman taking cover under a nearby chair. Everybody except Tight dress. People are pointing and laughing in unity, scumbags and policeman alike. My parting contribution to this pressure cooker has been to let a little steam out and force a bit of bonding. At heart we are all alike, whatever side of law we fall on. We all like laughing at the less fortunate. The Dutch tramp must have been coming under heavy fire in his dream, and everybody knows if you die in your dreams then you really do pop your clogs, so I've probably done him a favour. Think about something else. I don't really know what I'm doing; as it looks like Tight dress is getting booked in, so it's not like we could pop out for a drink anyway. I'm always like this after a night on the sauce. It's probably for the best – I already stand a pretty good chance of catching Hepatitis at work, without dipping myself into a disease-ridden honey pot out of it, however gorgeous she might be. I tell myself that this is one port I should definitely *not* dock in, even in a storm.

A queer fish:

Once out into the street, my hangover plucks up the courage to bully some bile from my gallbladder, and I have to swallow it out of politeness to my captor who now introduces himself as 'Landlubber'. I suppose it makes sense that he has a good sense of humour, in order to have let me off so easily. This is not a characteristic I have encountered in many policemen when they have been challenging me for pissing in the street. Once outside the station's entrance Landlubber tells me that he truly understands the pressures of my job, and assures me that he has no intention of grassing me up to my Governor. Stood here in uniform, his earnest compassion, penchant for Shakespeare, and his gentle humour seem like peculiar eccentricities for a Copper. This is all strangely good of him. I don't really understand why he is being so decent, when he could have made this difficult for me; I probably would do if the shoe was on the other foot. There is one caveat to his humanity however, that this little favour is a one-time only offer. I am warned to stay off the bottle and not be brought in again, or I can kiss my job goodbye. Landlubber shakes my hand, and I can feel that there is something pressing into my palm. He continues imprisoning my grip and raises his eyebrows indicating that he is waiting for me to acknowledge his ultimatum. I tell him quickly that's it's a done deal, and seeing as he hasn't let go of my hand I shake his again. Landlubber smiles and lets go, turns and walks back through the security door. My vision is still a little fuzzy due to this severe hangover that is cranking up through the gears, and it is a little difficult to focus on the small font on the card that I find in my newly released palm, so I pocket it for attention later.

Keelhauling:

I reach home from the police station early evening to bang up for the night. My feet are sore from the 12 mile flagellation walk I have punished myself with. I calculate this is the distance home, albeit it as the crow flies, according to a scale bus map I passed on route, although that does not take into account the three pubs I had to stop at to use the toilet, ask directions and have an emergency sandwich. Think about something else. These 12 miles equate to approx. 10.4 nautical miles which I can round down to 10. This pleases me. I like round numbers. I think I am going to dock home with an average speed of about four miles an hour, which I reckon is about 3.5 knots. I do these little conversions just to keep my hand in, and keep it fluid for when I need it. The monthly boat maintenance magazines I order make it almost impossible to open my front door. Like a barricade. I step onto the mat to de-character. I take the change out of my pocket, count it, react, and empty it into the demi-john to the right of the door. I unlace my boots and tie them together before dropping them over the handle of the small open window – which overlooks the fire escape leading up to the flat. I undo my belt, roll it up, and place it on the table next to the demi-john, in the compartment marked belt. I take my key chain out of my pocket and place that in its compartment, making sure each tally is visible on the end to prevent my hunting for them in the morning. I am not good in the mornings, so everything needs to be made as easy as possible. I take my ID wallet out, place this on the table, then my house keys on top. Same as always. I take my trousers off, fold and roll them into a sausage. I peel my sweat-wet socks and boxers off and throw them on top of my sausage. I take my epaulettes off and place them on the table, in their compartment. I unclip my tie from my collar, roll it up and place it on the table. Finally I take off my shirt, and roll it like a white skin round my sausage, then drop it into the laundry basket on the left of the door, on top of two other sausages. I am a little confused for a second, until I realise that was Yesterday's sausage. I knew it wasn't Wednesday.

Paul McMahon – Dead Reckoning

Standing naked, I pause for a moment and look around the flat. I look at the pictures of sailing boats, Toppers, Ribs, Knot diagrams, and coastline maps that adorn my walls, amongst a whole lot else, and breathe it all in. I find the images soothing and the notion of being coastal transports my soul out of this city and its moral vacuum. I walk into the lounge and close out Clapham High Street by dropping the sash, then press play on the stereo and wait patiently on Nick Drake. I'm horribly surprised then when Ray Charles pipes up, the same way I react when I mistakenly neck orange juice from the fridge instead of milk in the dark of the night. Put out, I turn toward the kitchen and focus my attention on the fridge, and in turn, the smell that is emanating from a small white bag I brought off the fish man at my local some days ago. The sea food has been in there too long, and one can't be too careful with cockles and shrimps. I reluctantly empty the contents into a bin liner and go back through the front room to put the rubbish by the front door. These things usually happen in threes. On returning through the front room I hit delete on the flashing answer machine, as I don't want to risk my precarious mood - nobody ever rings me with good news anyway. I let the kitchen door slam on Ray behind me. On opening the freezer I select a frozen meal - Lamb Hotpot - and put it in the microwave. The prisoners were having lamb stew from the hotplate yesterday for lunch and I had been looking forward to it all day.

Sacred Cow:

Dinner over, I throw the empty plastic bowl in the waste bin, and lean back in my arm chair. This is my favourite thing. This chair. I must have sat on thousands. I have argued with proprietors about the ergonomics of their favourite pieces, as well as non-ergonomic functional requirements: size, stackability, foldability, weight, durability, stain resistance and artistic design. I can state to you - the two most important anthropometric measurements for chair design: the popliteal height and buttock popliteal length. This chair has neither. It is a mystery why I love it so. It is from another age. It smells like history, and is so comfy English is incapable of exclaiming how. I live here because of this chair. All offers to buy it as a separate deal were rebuffed by the Landlady, a Mrs. Porter, at my first viewing of this hovel seven years previous. She insists they are not to part. Bitch. So here I am, living somewhere not entirely of my choosing.

A sop for Cerebus:

The Ray Charles CD ends. I get up from my chair, and wander over to the stereo. Incidentally this is also where I keep my spirits. My music collection shares the same cabinet as my alcohol. There is no point hiding it away; if you can't see it, it is less of an achievement. I flick through Chet Baker, Led Zeppelin, Miles Davis, The Velvet Underground, Nirvana, John Martin, and Pink Floyd. I try to think where Jim Morrison would be, he surely wouldn't have shacked up with Joni Mitchell. I decide enough is enough. I must sort the cases out, and what better time than the present. I begin to swap the cases around so that all house the correct CD. This done, I stand and look at them a while. Next I decide to arrange them all into alphabetical order, to aid the locating of Jim next time. This done, I pause a second time. I then pull all the CDs to the edge of the shelf so they are flush and level with each other. I look over my work. Thinking perhaps I am missing a few I count them slowly from the left to the right. Then, just to double check, I count them from the right to the Left. Then I pour a Bourbon.

Paul McMahon – Dead Reckoning

Enough rope to hang yourself:

I am a little irritable this morning as I have a headache; I am tired, and I am extremely dehydrated. All of these little sufferances, amplify my exasperation over the fact my bag is not being handed back to me with the speedy inefficiency that I would like it to be during this rare planned staff search into work. Instead this Mediterranean Officer, who doesn't normally even work here, is going through my possessions carefully. Not simply looking through them, but searching them. He actually opens my lunch box. He opens a fucking transparent lunch box, and moves around my salad with a latexed finger, eyeing each cherry tomato like it might pose a threat to national security. Actually searching on a staff search is a new development in our security procedures, which hitherto has consisted of a quick rummage around in your bag and turning out your pockets. There must be something in the offing. Now I don't like salad at the best of times, let alone when some fucker has had his digits amongst my leafage, but I can't blow up. If I look angry then everybody will *know* that I am angry, and who gets angry when people search them? Guilty fuckers. So, even if this arsehole wants to crack open my croutons and search them at molecular level, I can't say a fucking word to him without looking like I have something to hide. Which I don't.

Apparently I do have something to hide. This Mediterranean searching my stuff, mumbles something 'accenty', to the Senior Officer, who bounces over enthusiastically and peers into my bag.

There is a   . After a moment, both men then raise their glances to me in simultaneous horror as if they have just found a child's head at the bottom of my bag. The two staff either side of him stop searching their bags and lean over to look into mine. I am beginning to get a little panicky now for although I own many things inappropriate to bring into work, such as ninja stars from Thailand and a pretty dodgy DVD that I haven't

Paul McMahon – Dead Reckoning

watched all the way through from Peckham, I cannot for the life of me think what it is that is stopping my clean passage into work.

The Mediterranean slowly begins to pull out the 'unauthorised article' from within my bag. To the sound of gasps from the other searchers he holds aloft, for all to see, a piece of rope, and then brandishes it at me. Not a long length of rope. A piece. Of rope. A small, section of climbing rope - that I am using to practise my Knots with. This length of rope isn't of the necessary proportions to make the term 'escape equipment' even remotely applicable to it, unless you were a mouse and you were stuck in a biscuit tin. The S/O glares at me, demanding an explanation anyway. So I give him one; I simply announce calmly that I am going to tie the 'Turks Head' with it.

On the ropes:

There is uproar. The Mediterranean officer recoils in shock. The S/O starts flapping his arms around, ordering me in the back room immediately, away from accented shouts of 'racist'. A second later he marches in accompanied by the Security Governor who has been supervising the search, with my piece of rope in an evidence bag. The Governor asks me why I made such a deliberately provocative comment in front of the ethnic searching officer, whose release from his establishment to assist in this staff search was personally managed by the Security Governor. I am aware, without the Governor having to tell me, that the officer is only doing his job, and does not deserve racial taunts from anybody, let alone a fellow member of staff, but he tells me anyway. When the Governor has pauses to take a breath, I butt in explaining that the 'Turks Head', is actually a Knot.

Actual Conversation No. 1

Security Governor: A knot?

Me: Yes, Sir, 'The Turk's Head'.

Security Governor: Which you're claiming is a...?

Me: Knot. Yes, Sir. Of surprising complexity.

Security Governor: Assuming for a millisecond, that this isn't the worst excuse I have ever heard, why the hell would you be wanting to tie this knot?

Me: It is the best knot for reinforcing a cracked oar, or paddle sir?

Security Governor: And are you intending to go sailing up the Wings landing's today?

Me: You don't need oars when sailing Sir, and No, Sir.

Money for old rope:

In light of the circumstances and the Governors bulging vein, I feel it advisable to enlighten him, as to my full membership of the International Nautical Knot Tyres Guild. Seeing as how the Governor doesn't make any sort of reply, I carry on with a few facts that he may or may not find interesting. I tell him that, as far as I am aware, there are only around a thousand members globally, and that the majority of the committee are located in the UK as opposed to the USA.

Nothing.

Paul McMahon – Dead Reckoning

I don't know if the Governor is interested or not, as he is open mouthed, motionless, and isn't speaking. No one is speaking, so I carry on speaking. I explain to him that I am studying nautical knots, and occasionally take a piece of rope around with me to help me conquer the more challenging knots, so as to allow quick periods of practise when the opportunity presents itself.

Still nothing.

In an attempt to highlight the smallness, and therefore the insignificance of the rope, I explain how last year before the annual conference I was carrying two sections of rope about a metre long, in each pocket everywhere I went to practise the 'Chain Splice', as the fastest and best tied knot at conference fetches a financial prize. The Governor is rubbing his eyes with the base of his palms, and shaking his head. I have run out of knot trivia to distract the Governor with, and am left to suffer the awkward silence, and so I wait for the Governor to say something. He doesn't. What he does is waves both of his palms at me, shaking his head, and walks off back towards the search area again, leaving the S/O to take up the reigns. The S/O pushes the evidence bag against my chest, lets it go, and it slips down into my cupped hands below. The S/O stands still for a second looking at the floor, despondent. After a pause he sighs and tells me that he really thought they had something there. It's clear to me now that they are after somebody. We must be harbouring a wrong'un in our ranks. I ask the S/O what they're after today, and he tells me it's the same as always. Drugs, it surely has to be drugs. I hope they get caught whoever they are. Fucking arseholes. The S/O takes a deep breath in and puffs, shaking his head in disappointment, before looking up at me and chuckling again, and saying something I can't quite make out about being 'inland'.

His chuckling is interrupted by some radio traffic that only he can hear through his ear piece. He pushes his radio send button, and tells the control room that he will 'dispatch a team' straight away to the Control & Restraint storeroom. Due to me being one of the first ones in on shift, and being that I am stood right in front of him, it looks highly possible that the team he is about to dispatch is likely to have me in it. It does. I am told to report straight to the C & R storeroom and get 'kitted up' as one of the prisoners is kicking off in the segregation unit, and he is off, without so much as an apology or a good morning.

Close Quarters:

I am waiting to start this planned intervention that I have apparently 'volunteered' for, on a prisoner who I am now told has a knife and who I can hear shouting things I don't understand from the cell opposite. We have taken refuge in this empty cell facing the target cell on this side of the landing whilst the nurse, chaplain, member of IMB, and somebody who has the advanced technical capability to press a button on a video camera are found. There is always so much waiting to be done at times when so much action is required. Every incident feels like it's the first one the governors have ever had to organise. In the absence of anything to do, I look around the cell and ponder how it might feel to be banged up in here. I suppose I was pretty close to getting banged up properly last night, so a little soul searching might not be a bad use of this dead time. The first thing that strikes me from this slumped sitting position on the floor is the size. It really is very small indeed.

There is, however, no statutory minimum size for existing prison cells in the UK. I only know this little nugget of information because I have been told so by Shepard. Shepard is a serial litigant prisoner banged up on my wing, and he is an authority on prison law because he has an awful lot to complain about. Shepard tells me that despite this devious omission of a mandatory cell dimension in law, the Prison Service operating standards *do* lay down an *'ideal'* minimum size of 5.5 square metres. The one set of precise legal stipulations in existence regards the elements of a cell, which form the basis of most of his complaints, are mentioned only in Section 14 of the Prisons Act 1952, which requires cells to be 'certified' as being fit as regards their "size, lighting, heating, ventilation, & fittings". This keeps Shepard busy. Apparently, under PSO 1900, the certifying of prisoner accommodation is a job *so* important that it cannot be delegated, and is the sole responsibility of the Area manager. It is not unreasonable to conclude therefore that the Area manager has never actually been to this establishment, or if he has, he has never made it past coffee in the boardroom, due to the fact that we are still open and functioning.

This cell is typical for old Victorian-built prisons like this one. It's in a state of ill repair and is crawling with filth. But mainly, It's tiny, like a cabin. The cell size is a battle Shepard confesses to be losing. He has a complaint reply pinned to his cell notice board that I see every day and know word for word.

Exhibit A Cell A-2-36

Dear Mr Shepard,

Thank you for your complaint.

I am sorry that you feel the establishment is not providing you with the accommodation you feel you are entitled to.

I am afraid however that this establishment cannot be blamed for the human race evolving into taller species over the last 150 years, and that the 4" average height increase in natives of industrialised nations cannot be attributed to a conspiracy by the Ministry of Justice to cause prisoners' distress.

I hope this address your complaint to your satisfaction.

Regards,

No.1 Governor

The resin floor is coming up at the front corner behind this toilet, due to the corrosive volume of urine that is misfired on it daily. There is no toilet seat. Not a whole one any way, a shard is left, spiking out from the left hinge in search of a naïve buttock. There is a loo roll dangling off a ripped bed sheet attached to a small cupboard that has been jammed between the toilet and the bunk bed opposite as a makeshift privacy screen. The cupboard has no doors, and no back, as these have been ripped out to use as shelves in the opposite corner, rendering it effectively see-through. The bed is so close to the toilet that you could conceivably reach through the cupboard and flush the toilet in your sleep. The bunk bed that the cupboard is pushing against is leaning squew-iff against the far exterior wall, which is supporting its weight and preventing its collapse. On top of this most unstable of beds, lie two ripped mattresses and one pillow, all on the top bunk. Nothing on the bottom. The cell smells. I would push the window open further myself, passed the limits of the bracket to let a little more air in, if it had not been broken this way already. It doesn't help that there are so many people in here, not to mention the thick material I am dressed up in.

I am kitted out in my full personal protective equipment, except my helmet which is lying on the floor at my feet with the only single slash resistant glove I can find stuffed inside, and minus my stab vest which is too bloody small to actually get into, and my leg guards which have no Velcro to keep them in place anyway but, apart from that, I am wearing the rest of my uniform protective equipment. By rest, I mean my thick cotton boiler suit, which is what is making me so bloody hot. There is still nothing happening and the heat is making me extremely sleepy under this thick cotton 'body armour'.

zzzzzzzzzzzzzzzzzzzzzzzzzzzzzzzzzzzzzzzzzzzzzzzzzzzzzzzzzzz zzzzzzzzzzzzzzzzzzz

Gav wakes me up. My neck is a little sore from the position I have drifted off in, and my back is hurting as I am leant up against a shield. Although I can't look up due to my cricked neck, I can tell it is Gav who has woken me up because his distinctive boots are in my eye line. Individual, so they are; as they haven't seen a polish since the factory and smell worse than a rotting seagull.

Actual conversation No.2

Gav: Oi 'Defecator', are you sober?

Me: Its 08:45!

Gav: So? You fell over when we was getting changed!

Me: I'm knackered, you lemon; it's what happens to people who work a full week without going sick.

Gav: Dickhead.

Me: Prick.

Gav explained:

Gav's jowls are remarkable for a man in his 30's, as is his ability to engage in any task with a B & H hanging out of his mouth. He is shorter than me, which I appreciate, and slightly more rotund than me as he is carrying a little holiday weight apparently, although I am not sure from which year. His features are dark, two Brown eyes, 31 brown teeth and thousands of black hairs which have a head start on receding.

Gav speaks with a pseudo-cockney accent. His parents were part of the mass exodus of middle class white folks from London to Kent, prompted by the favourable house prices and the influx of "Fucking Albanians in the 80s", and as a second generation Sidcupion he reclaims with vigour every syllable his "Old Dear" left behind in the "Old Smoke". He and I met at training, and have shared a healthy arse covering comradery ever since. His career has thus far consisted of part active service and part suspension, in equal measure. We are true friends most certainly, but I have no idea why.

"Mfumbuaii ansi!"

Gav brings me up to date reference the briefing that I have missed whilst snoozing. Apparently the *"Dirty African Bastard"* is playing up, and the S/O has finally got a "fourf man for the team, so we're ready naa". The *'DAB'*, is apparently threatening staff and playing up. By playing up Gav actually means shitting up. This involves smearing faeces over ones self, the observation glass, and the general area of the cell - officially named 'Dirty Protest'. It is unfortunate according to Gav, that we only have The *'DAB'* on a dirty protest. Had we a second, we could have merely swapped their cells over should they have refused to come off voluntarily.

Paul McMahon – Dead Reckoning

He goes on to posit that everybody likes the smell of their own shit, and points out quite rightly that this unusual appreciation does not extend to a whiff of someone else's.

I have had more than my fair share of faeces over the last 24 hours, and am trying not to see the obvious parallels between our situations. Now I have my helmet on, I note how strong my breath smells of Bourbon as the aroma is reflected back at my nostrils by the Perspex visor. Luckily the Bourbon masks the odour of 'feaceas-Africán'. I congratulate myself on this foresight and then quickly think about something else, leaving me feeling clever and one step ahead of the game. A neat little trick.

We are preparing to assault the cell and my team start to manhandle me into position. I take hold of Oily's belt, and tuck myself in behind him on his gargantuan right side. This is correct formation. This is also because he has a large shield. Gav tucks himself in directly behind Oily on his equally gargantuan left side. I haven't enquired as to the origin of Oily's nickname and decided long ago that I didn't want to know - In the same way as I don't want to know what is in 'Meat Paste'. They can both remain non-descript and a mystery as far as I'm concerned, especially when I feel this bad. The 'Forf man' looks into the cell through the observation glass, and passes the message to us that he can, "…see nothing through the shit". Oily thanks him for his insightful comments. Gav follows up with a jibe about his forward thinking strategy. I make do with a laugh. I am not feeling my best. The forf man is 'Gollum'. A disgrace to the uniform. I don't know what his real name is. He's not got enough time in service for me to use it anyway. So, Gollum it is. It fits - ugly little bastard. The service really must be scraping the barrel if he's turned up on scene. Gollum has the enviable job of being the 'leg man'. This means he does Fuck all, save lay on the legs once we have the inmate under control. Even Gollum couldn't fuck that up. True to form, he looks like a total twat today. He's picked up someone else's kit bag and has to keep pushing the oversize helmet back over his eyes. This is

Paul McMahon – Dead Reckoning

good. I feel the communal attention focus on him, and witness my odd little daytime kip evaporate from the collective mind of the group.

The '*DAB*' is swearing - presumably. In some dialect or another. A pointless folly if the nominated victim of your slur can't understand what you're saying. Nevertheless he really is going for it. An order is given for him to uncover the observation glass, and move to the back of the cell. He briefly breaks into English -

The DAB: Fuck Yor!

Fuck yor...? It is unclear if either party understands what is being asked of them. The order is then given to enter the cell. This part all goes very fast. It always does. Once the team has begun to enter, that's it. You've had your chance. It would be pointless raising your hands, changing your mind or begging. Yippiekiyay-Mother-Fucker. In for a penny in for a pound. In for a Rupee in for a Rand. The cell door is opened and Oily turns the shield slightly to the right, unsettling me as it exposes me for a moment, to enable us to fit through the door. He is moving at such a speed that I would be going with him whether I wanted to or not. The stench in here is overwhelming, mainly as the thermostat has been mischievously adjusted in an attempt to smoke him out, and this has ripened the smell somewhat. The '*DAB*' is perched on top of the stainless steel sink, resting on his heels like a coiled rattle snake. He leaps off his perch toward the oncoming Oily, which is unwise as it only serves to intensify the impact. His trajectory changes upon meeting our shield, and he is pushed back with a similar speed into the sink he departed a split second ago, expelling an unworldly sound. There is no African translation for hindsight - I have checked. The remainder of the relocation is very much cut and dry. He is wrapped up, and placed in Locks, then transferred into a fresh cell. En route me and Gav attempt to out-do each other, each taking it in turns to emit as loud a sound from our instrument as possible, I

Paul McMahon – Dead Reckoning

playing a right arm, and Gav playing a left. Serves him right for shitting up. Dirty bastard.

I have to admit I am enjoying this a little bit, only because Gav is having such a good time and laughter is infectious. All this physical exertion is causing me to over-heat a little bit, and booze is steaming through my pours like a distillery. I wish the *DAB* would have a little consideration and stop requiring so much effort to control him. I shout at Gollum to make himself useful and raise my visor to allow some cool fresh air to flow into my face, making it easier to breathe and see what I am doing, as my steamed-up visor is dripping in condensation from my breath, making it impossible to see without wiping it; which I would do if I didn't have a wriggling African to subdue.

$(x -h)^2 + (y -k)^2 = r^2$

The method behind achieving passivity and submission in a prisoner is to simply apply pain to them until they stop resisting, and then stop applying pain. This approach is enshrined in law as the use of force must be 'proportionate' and 'necessary', according to PSO 1600 and a little inconvenient thing called the European Convention of Human Rights. The principle is easy enough for me to comprehend:

1. (x) Struggle + (y) pain application = (c) compliance.

However, due to Gav's natural propensity toward violence, and thanks in part to my bag search this morning, the invisible formula we seem to be currently applying to the problem can be more accurately represented as-

Paul McMahon – Dead Reckoning

1. (x) Struggle = (c) compliance + (y) pain application

I have discussed Gav's unique approach to restraint with my homeless friend Melvin over a late night purple can on the steps outside the tube station, and he explains that Gav manages to ensure compliance is an equal radius from both pain application and struggle at all times. I am not numerically equipped to argue. If I had been good with numbers maybe I'd have been a navigator and not a prison officer.

Nobody is aware of the current presence and use of this clandestine formula. Not the video camera, not the Governor, or any of the medical staff, or even the Independent Monitoring Board member who is eagle eyeing the goings on. The only people who are aware are myself, Gav, the DAB - and a solitary face pressed up against the observation panel peering out at me from a cell directly in front of me.

Regio facialis

I am immediately uncomfortable. I have my visor up, and my face is clearly visible as I am not wearing my balaclava. This is due to the fact that there hasn't been any kit replaced in the store room since the dawning of time. Now this would be reason alone to be a little perturbed, in case my identity gets back to the prisoner being restrained, or a motivated associate, but what makes it even more awkward is that in the moment our eyes meet I am caught having a bloody good laugh. I am smiling ear to ear, caught up in the indulgence of the moment. Cavorting around the floor with my mate, seemingly inflicting gratuitous violence against a poor undeserving prisoner; at least that's how I imagine the face is seeing it.

Paul McMahon – Dead Reckoning

This face is unfortunately more than just a random physiognomy. Unfortunately it belongs to Tigger, a prisoner normally located on my Wing. I know he has been down here for some time after he was nicked for failing a Mandatory Drugs Test. I stop in my tracks and he holds my stare without saying a word. At this point Gollum slams the flap on the observation panel, a split second before I break Tigger's gaze in shame. I would have liked Tigger to have seen this modicum of regret. Gollum can't do anything right; the flaps should have been shut from the bloody outset, and if they weren't the least he could have done is have the sort of sixth-sense perceptiveness which could allow me to affect a moment of reconciliation. Prick.

Conscience

Gav tells me I need to go and get some sleep. He says I should go home sick, that I should never have come in on my week off anyway, regardless of the overtime, and that I "Look like shit". I consult my conscience…

1. Not one manager has asked if I'm okay after this *incident*.

2. No one has told me I may go for a shower after all that shit…

3. I haven't been given my half hour stand down time after being involved in control and restraint as per PSO 1600.

Paul McMahon – Dead Reckoning

Therefore I decide to my surprise I *can* go home, uncharacteristically, on the grounds I have been injured in the removal of the *'DAB'*. Plausible. Think about something else. As it turns out I am too worried about leaving them short. Gav catches me walking back from the gate to the wing five minutes after he escorted me there, and reminds me how bad I stink, and that "Governor Cunt's on duty". It is his turn to wink at me. That's my way out! I whip out my personal POA diary into which I have pasted multiple sections of a variety of PSO's that I feel I need to have permanent instant access to:

Mandatory actions

1. *If a manager has reasonable cause to suspect that a member of staff may have breached the standards set out in PSO 8610, they must inform the Duty Governor or Head of Group who will consider whether a breathalyser test is appropriate to confirm the suspicion.*

I convince myself that I would be found out and in turn I would be suspended, that they would be unable to cope on the Wing, and the prison would crumble into chaos; ultimately I need to go home for the good of my colleagues. I turn and walk back towards the gate full of morality, slowly incorporating a limp. Slight at first, though by the time I arrive at the front gate, I look like I should be in casualty. I give an obligatory suck of air through my teeth, like a cowboy plumber weighing up a price on a u-bend, and wince a little as I stop to throw my keys down the chute. Once my numbered tallies have been issued in exchange, I nod at the gate man, proudly limp out of the Prison, and hobble down the road.

Paul McMahon – Dead Reckoning

Anchor home:

I jump off the bus at the stop after mine and halt to do up my pre-undone shoelace to covertly observe if anybody got off the bus with me. Being that I work in a local Remand prison, if you get arrested, are remanded, on trial, convicted, or on local discharge, in this post code or any of the surrounding postcodes, or you have a case in any of the many courts in this area, then you are extremely likely to meet me in person. Being that there is such a high crime rate in this area, and specifically on my road, I calculate that the chances of me bumping into an ex-con, or one observing me enter my home are pretty high, and so precautionary measures must be taken. There is however right now there is only one old man, walking in the other direction, who was on my bus, so I begin to walk the short distance back toward my flat. Before pushing the lower courtyard door open, I can make out the sound of some forlorn character emoting some serious depression-acting from Nick's TV in the ground floor flat. He loves his weirdly dark B movies, that lad. I slip unnoticed past the door and up to the flat. Once I have tossed the sausage, I run a bath to remove the stench. Stench removing is not simple however, as I don't have many products in the bathroom. In fact I don't have much of anything in the bathroom. I don't have an obligatory duck even. I do however have a floating mini replica of the Cutty Sark.

Vestis verum reddit

I arrive at the front door early this morning. My ablutions were thorough: Shit, shower, and shave. I am wearing a crisp, ironed uniform and smell like I am going for an interview. I collect my Kit in reverse order, and do my belt up an extra notch; there will be nothing slack about me today. Lets have it you bastards. I lock the door behind me and run down the fire escape. Down to Nick and his rats. I suppose they're *all our* rats but they're most

Paul McMahon – Dead Reckoning

audible in his flat. His front door is wide open as always. I peek my head round the door and say hi. He is lying on the floor in amongst take away cartons. This makes me feel very good about myself. Fucking waster. I up my tempo and bound out the bottom door.

The journey in to work is uneventful. I make an effort to be pleasant to the bus driver, who does not appreciate it. I make a note of his face in case he makes an appearance at work one day soon. He will not ruin this for me. I 'dry clean' my route to throw off any tail, by swapping buses at of my usual spot and go out of my way to be rude to the driver of the 159. I have successfully handed on something I was passed. Balance restored I jump off two stops early and walk with purpose the rest of the way. God help the Con's today.

I enter the gate and toss my tallies down the chute. The gate man looks at me, nods and points at his leg in surprise. It is too late for that now. I am a quick healer and that is that. Think about something else. I collect my keys and attach them to my chain whilst heading for the last electric gate. I arrive on the wing early to take the helm and relieve the night patrol, who is particularly happy to see me. The wing is now mine. I sit on the front desk and check the role. It is 264. I check the detail and see I am working the 3s. I check the 3s roll and see it is 76. I note I am working with Gav today. I am about to go into the office when an emergency cell bell 'buzzer' goes. It is coming from 3-33. I check the roll board and see the occupants are Winnie Jr, a tosser, and LaPorte; a nobody. I start up the stairs to the 3s and begin to feel fresh. I approach the cell door of 3-33, and slam the observation flap open.

Actual conversation No.3

Me: What's the emergency?

Nobody: Me a need a Rizzla from next door Gov.

Me: Are you bleeding?

Nobody: No!?

Me: Suicidal?

Nobody: Me a want a Rizzla Gov!

Me: Do I look like a fucking corner shop, to you Mug? I might be wearing black and white but I'm not your fucking butler. Right, Cunt?

Nobody falls silent. I shut the flap with the same force I opened it with. I shall be nothing but consistent today, and walk off, listening for a retort. Nothing from nobody. As I reach the 2s, Bailey calls from his single cell:

Bailey: Mr B, is on one today star!"

Yes. Yes I am.

I Photocopy five nicking sheets, for I feel I may need them today, collect some latex gloves, retrieve my stave from the bottom of my locker, and wait the arrival of the others. The first to arrive is Gav. He walks into the office, looking pissed off as usual, throws a fag at me, and his Matrix coat over the door. Then slumps into one of the four 'comfy' chairs, I am on the office 'Talbot recliner', a

Paul McMahon – Dead Reckoning

mass-produced but well-built padded swivel chair with height and back adjustment levers. I tell him we are working together today, which cheers him up. He lifts an invisible pint glass and toasts the 8:00 dropping.

It has come to pass, that on most mornings for about a month when the wing was bad, we would open our landing with some resident inmates who had been received from F- wing late the previous day. They had not yet had the pleasure of our company. These prisoners arrive with a very bad attitude, and a misguided opinion of the staff on this wing; specifically the 3s. We would spend the first 15 minutes of the morning ascertaining who had arrived with 'F-Wing Fever' and making sure it was exorcised out of them publicly, and immediately. It's not hard to spot; giveaway symptoms' include eyeballing staff, bowling down the middle of the landing topless, insults, and a general misguided belief that they are in charge. By 08:00 every morning there would be a guaranteed alarm bell on A- Wing. For those inmates who had been there a while, and for whom it had also happened to, it became a spectator sport and a source of amusement to start their day on, watching the clueless newbies strut around, and bet on who would be first to bite - and in turn hit the floor.

Stockholm Syndrome

I have only to keep this up for one day as I have volunteered to take an unwanted set of nights, and therefore have no more day shifts this week after 17:30 hrs today. I'm explaining the change in legislation to a small Jamaican man who wants to try and claim his days in police custody back, the upshot of it being that he isn't going to get them because his offence was committed *after* April 2003, blah, blah, blah… Hence his release date *is* correct. I'm not concentrating on what I am saying really; I've repeated the same stock answer over and over to men of all shapes, sizes, creeds and countries. He thanks me and begins to leave, crossing the threshold of my Wendy house, then he turns and tries to ask something about his canteen…

Actual Conversation No.4

Me: Sorry, I'll have to stop you there – there is only one enquiry per day allowed. If you want anything else you'll have to write it down and put it in the out-of-hours application box.

Nohope: Can I have an application then?

Me: No. Only one request per day I'm afraid.

Nohope: How do I get one of them forms then?

Me: You'll have to put in an application…

I usher in the next man waiting in line, and get him to close the door on the confused Jamaican. I have to spread myself around 76 people's problems today, and save a little time for the real work. No time for this. He wanders over to Gav, and I watch him through the glass as he asks him something - he really stands no chance of a straight answer out of Gav. Further down the landing, my No.1 cleaner; 'Chucky' makes a 'T' sign; I raise my thumb. Good Lad. ChuckyiIs a small Londoner with a big walk. His "…other 'alf is banged up in 'ollaway", and for a phone call to her unit he is a most dedicated man.

Paul McMahon – Dead Reckoning

Prison is psychological warfare for an officer. Everybody wants a piece of you. No conversation, or gesture is real. Everybody has an agenda; the universe in a microcosm - and desperate. You are these people's confidant, jailor, postman, friend, lifeline, nemesis, bread winner and provider. Save a mutiny, you are their Captain. It is a fine balancing act. Prison is run on the good will of the inmates. Simple maths ratio. You do not bite the hand that feeds you, the hand that gives you your letter from home, the hand that, for the moment, holds the key. I raise two fingers in a V, and mouth "two sugars". Good lad.

Sisyphean toil:

My patience playing the bank manager runs out and I stop explaining half way through in the third different way I know how, why A4765AL Kafka isn't missing £2.50 on his prison account. I unplug the computer and the screen clunks off. I stand and usher him out of the lean-to. Nodding my head at Gav playing pool, I make my way toward today's unlucky first quarter. The landing is lined on each side with cells, and is then split in four by two shower recesses in the middle of each side. Each of these is a quarter. I am about to start the bread and butter of the job, owning the landing. Every day I enter each cell on the landing, quarter by quarter, and check the physical fabric of the cell, the walls, widows, bars, etc. I ensure that each inmate has only the designated amount of kit: one towel, one cabinet, one blanket, one plate, etc. I remove any excess kit and have it returned to the store man on the bottom landing, ready for the process of begging, borrowing, and stealing to begin all over again. This will happen every day, for eternity, and I shall not bore of it. This is an important ritual. It is not simply an extra sheet, it a symbol of my authority on this vessel. It is a reason to enter each cell and nose around, to mark my territory. There are no

Paul McMahon – Dead Reckoning

blind spots on the 3s. There are no out of bounds areas here. This is my world. My world.

Miss Bezonian:

On route I look over the landing at whats-er-name on the 1s. I can't understand what she keeps jolting up at. I stop and concentrate hard. After a while I match her reaction to that of the dominoes slamming into the pool table cover on the 2s. The jungle drums. I think *I* would find it unsettling if they *weren't* there. I make myself a promise to find out her name later. After I have done this.

Touch wood:

It looks like Gav wants to do the LBB's now. As I arrive he is already gloved up and pacing outside 3-01. He seems quite keen to get on with them, which is odd as Gav's not keen on being keen. Some days we proceed methodically doing a cell at a time together, and other days we piggyback each other, doing a cell on our own, and hopping over each other all the length of the landing like today, as this is evidently how Gav wants to do it. He is mixing it up, no problem; I am a fan of keeping the regular irregular as far as the prisoner's world is concerned, it keeps them on their toes. As I've finished in 3-17, I approach the door way to leave. I see Gav walking past the cell I'm in. He continues past 3-18 toward 3-19, meaning I have to alter the natural rhythm of our working and do 3-18, which he has missed out for some reason. I enter 3-18 and quickly smack the window bars with my hand to check that they are still in one piece and head straight back out the door pressing the emergency cell bell to check that it works. As I come out of the cell I press the reset button on the outside wall to turn of the horrendous beeping that the cell bell emits, and stop the annoying flashing light. Whilst I am doing this I see Gav at the door of 3-19, with his hand against the wall and peering into the cell through a hipflask-width gap in the cell door, which is ajar. Gav looks like he is trying to silently push the door open but the door is not keen to allow this. I am much heavier than Gav and so immediately push past him to the door, which doesn't appear to please him. He looks like he doesn't really want me there. He must want all the glory to himself. Selfish bastard. It occurs to me that Gav must have known there was something going on in here as we approached the cell, although I have no idea how. I admire him for this degree of awareness.

There is a cabinet in front of the door. This type of make-shift barricade is designed only as a stalling method to give the occupants enough time to squirrel away any contraband before a member of staff or another prisoner makes entrance to the cell. I have seen this a million times before.

Actual conversation No 5 (Part 1):

Voice: Who it?

Me: Open…

Gav: …the FUCKING door.

Voice: Quick. Lose it Blood!

This is all I need.

Gav slams into the door sending me hinge-ward bound into the cell door frame. The barricade budges slightly and the door relinquishes a little ground. As Gav again slams into the door I flip open the cell observation panel in time to see the TV fly off the

Paul McMahon – Dead Reckoning

cabinet behind the door toward the floor. I can hear distinct voices telling us to calm down. This is one of life's paradoxes. The only thing which will make a person more epically angry than they are already are is being told to calm down. The reaction is predictable. With an irate almighty slam, the Kettle falls and I can hear the water splash, out of sight. The cabinet is bouncing now, and has chosen its side. It is trying to let us in, but is jammed against the toilet partition - an ill-fitted piece of wood, jutting out of the wall, modestly covering the toilet so as to give its occupant a little dignity from peering eyes. The situation is beyond placation now. The pool cues have been downed behind us on the landing, and the focus of the 3s crowd is firmly on the door way of 3-19. The abuse begins; a few faces begin to rally the masses, to incite a revolt. To tempt a riot. Gav does not know. He is in the zone; I too forget about the marauding crowd as Gav's venom is infectious. I can hear nothing now except my own voice unconsciously quoting the relevant charge like a perverted physical mantra, as I slam the full weight of my body into the door in synchronicity with Gav's.

Me: obSTRUct an OFFicer in the COUrse of his DUties

With the last syllable, the door flies open sending the kettle flying, and sound returns with enthusiasm. A2471CP is on the floor covered in hot water, having evidently chosen an unlucky place to sit, squealing like a piggy. Pink like one, too. The television sparks and crackles under foot. My speed carries me into A3490AP. He is at the back of the cell against the wall screaming Patwa with his hands down his trousers. This is where his hands stay, until I smash him into said wall, and they make a hasty manoeuvre to catch his tooth; I wonder if Jamaica has a cricket team – for he would make an excellent wicket keeper. Gav pulls 'Piggy' out to market and comes back into the cell approximately ten seconds later, by which

Paul McMahon – Dead Reckoning

point 'Wicket Keeper' is on the floor and I am standing in front of him. The alarm bell is sounding on my radio, and I wonder what is going on elsewhere in the Prison.

Actual conversation No. 5 (Part 2)

Gav: Get up

Wicket Keeper: Blood clart!

Me: Stand the fuck up when he speaks to you!

Wicket Keeper: Me don't respect him, he a pussy-'ole!

Gav: Up!

Wicket Keeper: Wha? Ya can't 'andle de opposition?...

At this juncture it apparently becomes necessary for Gav to deliver a quick blow to whence the incomprehensible twaddle is coming from.

Wicket Keeper: Please Gov man.

Me: Now...Stop bleeding on my fucking floor and stand up.

Wicket Keeper: I'm up.

Gav: Now give it here.

Paul McMahon – Dead Reckoning

(Prisoner holds out his bloody tooth)

Gav: Not your tooth, you docile cunt!

Wicket Keeper: Look a' me toot man.

Gav: Fuck your tooth. Give up the gear!

Wicket Keeper: Me got nothing Big man.

Gav clearly doesn't like this prisoner. He obviously knows something I don't, as I haven't picked up on anything that has caused me to want to inflict more than the staple amount of violence on him. But Gav has a keen eye for detail. What is strange is that the prisoner seems to dislike Gav a lot too. Much more than is usual, although it could just be a spontaneous reciprocation of Gav's overt display of loathing.

Gav goes behind 'Wicket Keeper', momentarily making *him* piggy in the middle. He does not nowhere to look. Gav' tells him he's going to be strip searched and off I go, switching passive aggressive professional like I'm reciting a page out a manual:

Paul McMahon – Dead Reckoning

Look to the left
Look to the right
Take shirt off.
R   a   I   s   e   a   r   m   s.
Tu
d   rn
n   ar
ou
Lower arms.
Put shirt on.
Boxers
Off
T   T
A   R
K   O
E   U
                     S
O   E
F   R
F   S
Socks   Off

Boxers off... at this point a cigarette-box sized, brown object drops from his boxers on to the cell floor. Gav picks it up instinctively, pockets it, and tells me it's cannabis. Gav informs the wicket keeper that he doesn't like being lied to via a punch to the face and a grab of the throat, and asks him if there is anything else in here he shouldn't have. Wicket Keeper splutters he has nothing else. As a point of thoroughness I tell Wicket Keeper to squat. Gav kindly assists him by letting him go. Wicket Keeper curtsies like a little girl. I tell him to stand with feet shoulder width apart and squat again, the purpose being to expel anything else he has tried to plug up his arse. He does a good impression of an elegant Victorian lady sitting, knees together. I sportingly offer Wicket Keeper one

Paul McMahon – Dead Reckoning

final chance to squat properly or hand over any unauthorised article, and tell him I will make sure the Governor knows 'how compliant he was' - which he refuses, before I grab hold of his head and bring him to the floor of 3-19, Using approved Control and Restraint techniques, Your honour.

Adding insult to injury:

In between guttural screams and winces of pain, Wicket Keeper suddenly cries out something intelligible amongst all the ensuing noise that is accompanying our scuffle about Gav being 'Bent'. I don't know what it is about Jamaicans and their obsession with the subject of male homosexuality. I can testify that this features heavily in their choice of preferred insults. I have been called a 'Battyman' and a 'chi-chi' man so often over the last few years that it occasionally slips into my own vernacular, and so I am not surprised to hear that, in his moment of red-handedness, he is casting aspersions on Gav's sexuality. This however is a mistake. There are suddenly fireworks going off behind Gav's eyes at the mention of the word. Gav is instantly one very angry young man. I'm not sure why, as 'bent' is a rather limp sort of abuse in truth, and not very *Jamaican* at all. I suppose it must be the fact that these prisoners have had the audacity to have such a large amount of resin out during full association that must have really upset Gav, and the accusation that he likes to fuck men has only served to infuriate him further. This job is lucky to have the likes of Gav, as he is evidently taking his job very seriously all of a sudden. Gav is going at Wicket Keeper like a man possessed.

Due to the code of honour amongst us prison officers, I support Gav by raining in a few blows of my own, out of duty and in the spirit of solidarity. Wicket Keeper musically harmonises the low bassey thuds of our feet on his torso with some pitchy high falsetto. I guess we've made our point, so I stop and back off. Gav

Paul McMahon – Dead Reckoning

evidently hasn't made his point yet, and continues to make it over and over again. I think Wicket Keeper has got the message and put my hand on Gav's shoulder. He stops, and we all stay still for a second. I wander if Wicket Keeper is alive. Gav must also be wandering if he is alive, as he kicks him one last time to find out. Wicket Keeper recoils in pain, and I breathe a sigh of relief. I don't much fancy appearing in Coroner's Court if I can help it. That would be a bit of a sticky wicket.

I hear the familiar voice of Oscar 1over my shoulder, outside the cell. In unison both me and Gav fling ourselves down on top of Wicket Keeper, in order to get into the sort of position that we would be in if we had acted like we were supposed to up to this point. Oscar 1 puffs into the cell and manages to ask in between gasps what has happened. I briefly explain that "the prisoner had not complied with my instructions during a strip search, and it is my belief he has an unauthorised article secreted on his person, Sir". I also add that under prison Rule 47 I have the power to search the prisoner under restraint, in accordance with the Prisons Act 1952, and the Prison rules Act 1999. This makes me sound like a knob, as it is completely unnecessary, and all present are aware of the relevant legislation, I am sure. All the same it is very professional. I always retreat into the rule book when things get out of control. I wonder why Oscar 1 isn't at the alarm bell I heard on the radio. Gollum pushes into the cell, and takes 'control' of Wicket Keepers limp free arm, after faffing around with it for a few seconds like a retarded kid with a Rubik's Cube. Gollum screams "Lock on" ad looks proudly up at me. I note Gav's face. Oscar 1, pushes the door to, and in response to my nod at Wicket Keeper's arse, rips our toothless friend's boxers down. As is always the case when drugs are involved in prison, mobile phones are always lurking around as well. This is a real stroke off luck and will help in justifying the ever increasing number of bruises that are breeding exponentially over Wicket Keeper's exposed midriff before my very eyes. Oscar 1 takes hold of a tiny Panasonic mobile phone which is clearly strapped round the underside of Wicket

Paul McMahon – Dead Reckoning

Keeper's testes, by a novel use of an elastic band, and wrenches it off, almost taking a bollock with it. A beautiful manoeuvre. On exiting the cell I see the wing has been banged up. The A- Wing staff are cheery, as this means their association period has been cut short and a decision has been made to leave all the con's behind their doors till 'Feeding'. Wicket Keeper, takes a while to calm down. Once he has stopped screaming he is taken down to see the medic, reference his missing tooth, and bafflingly swollen testes. The look of abhorrence on his face is priceless when he is told he will have to wait until 'Piggy's burns have been treated - his pork crackling. Our S/O grunts his approval at me and tells us to get down the 'Seg' while it's quiet to do our paperwork for the 'dropping'. This is as much appreciation as his rank permits him to give, and as much as I need to make everything worthwhile. That and a pat on the back - out of view of Gollum. As Wicket Keeper is led away in cuffs, he glances up at Gav. I see Gav draw a mimed zip across his lips at him. I don't really think in light of the beating that he just got, that he would grass us up for distributing it to him for fear of another, but I suppose Gav must just be making sure.

Feeding time goes well on the 3s. Our landing is banged up and counted before the hotplate workers have even begun to take their food. The new F-Wing consignment on the 3s go behind their doors with ease, having been educated from afar. Gav confidently signs our numbers on the front desk without checking, and throws the pen nonchalantly down in the folder, much to the annoyance of Gollum who is still chasing prisoners around trying to get them behind their doors like a lame sheepdog.

It's pretty clear to me that Gav thinks he has gone a bit far today. He is being uncharacteristically quiet and offers to do all the evidence paperwork for the massive lump of cannabis he has in his pocket, so I don't have to do anything. I suppose this is his way of saying sorry for getting a bit carried away with the violence, as I know how much he hates writing out the evidence log and recording the particulars on the evidence bags. He always slopes this sort of thing off on me, so I am pleased that I won't have to spend time writing it all up on my own yet again. I appreciate this little show of repentance, and don't argue with Gav. I'll allow him to atone for bringing the spotlight on us in this way if he wants, and I don't say another word about it.

I lock the gate to A-Wing and shout my farewells to Gav and the rest of the lads who are staying for the evening duty shift. Today was just what I needed. Everything has been reassuringly predictable today. I have answered everything asked of me and have only referred to my pocket book twice for assistance - I hate to give out wrong information; It must cause a colleague some sort of problem down the line. My Landing has been cleaned, all equipment accounted for, and all have received meals. The post has been delivered and everybody knows where they stand. I have delivered a positive regime for my 76. No one has gone wanting. All needs have been met. My workers are content. Landing balance is intact. I am in the Gate lodge before I realise, and couldn't tell you how I got here. As I wait for the Drug Slot to drop their keys, I wonder what I will have to eat tonight. My cleaners said the curry was good. I think I have a Prawn Vindaloo in the freezer somewhere.

Sundowners syndrome:

When I get home I must remember to force myself to east something before I turn in for the day. This week of night shifts is going to upset my patterns. I will eat irregularly, experience gastrointestinal complaints, including constipation, excessive flatulence, abdominal pain and heartburn. I will get diarrhoea. I will find it hard to speak to people. I will develop shift lag. It will fuck with my body's circadian rhythm. When the normal circadian rhythms are disrupted by lack of sleep or by crossing time zones, it takes days or weeks to readjust. I may be left with sleep disorders, fatigue, heart disease and high blood pressure. I may become paranoid. Much more paranoid.

Fly in the ointment:

I am standing outside the door of my flat, searching for my keys. I close my eyes and can smell old harbour; discarded fishing vessels abandoned with half their haul intact. Smells like my flat is rotting. For some reason I knock on my door, in the vain hope I've not walked far enough up the fire escape. It's happened before, Nick has got the same front door, a Mrs thingy job lot, although he lives on the 1s - the garden flat. No one answers, so I open my eyes and fumble around for my keys once more. When I leave the prison, I usually swap them into the same pocket as my work keys live, but I must have been in a hurry. Finding them in my coat I open the door. I can't hear the high street from here. I must have left the sash windows closed. The flat is quiet apart from a faint buzzing. The buzzing gets a little nearer and two flies clumsily navigate around me and make their way out the door. Yesterday's seafood stinks at me, and I curse myself for forgetting the rubbish this morning.

Fly off the handle:

I pick it up and fling it over the fire escape loosely in the direction of the bin outside Nick's flat. I renter the flat and stand on the mat. I take the change out of my pocket and count it. React. Then drop it into the demi-john. I bend down and unlace my boots, take them off, then tie the laces together and drop them over the handle of the small window. As I begin to un-notch my belt, I can feel something seeping through my socks. I look down and see

Paul McMahon – Dead Reckoning

the mat is wet through. I take off my sopping socks and roll them together. I collect the mat, walk barefoot onto the fire escape and throw both items after my ex-dinner. I don't wait to see where they land. These things usually happen in threes.

Fly on the wall:

Sat naked in my chair I decide there's no point going to the CD cabinet. I know for a fact I don't own anything fitting to play now. I glance over at the answer machine and see that it is flashing again. I reach over and press play, uncharacteristically tempting fate.

"Hi Michelle…its Gemma…look don't take this the wrong way, but I don't want you to come tonight okay? I know we are sisters an' all but this is really important and I can't be made to look bad. This is a big night for me…okay?…I mean it… I don't want to see you there."

I feel myself becoming angry, more alive than I have all day. What a bitch. I can't let this pass. I press # on the phone key pad and listen to the BT lady tell me she is about to return the call.

*"Hello you've reached Danny and Gemma, sorry we're not available to take your call. Please leave a message after the tone, and one of us will give you a call back as soon as we can…..*beep.*"*

Paul McMahon – Dead Reckoning

I hang up the phone. That's is no good. I want to tell her, as an offended stranger. How dare she. Poor Michelle…whoever she is. I walk over to the CD cabinet and pour a small(ish) whiskey. Tonight doesn't count. I have had a productive day. I walk back to the answer machine and press # once more.

*"Hello you've reached Danny and Gemma, sorry we're not available to take your call. Please leave a message after the tone, and one of us will give you a call back as soon as we can…..*beep.*"*

I pause for a moment.

A little flap of the butterfly's wings.

"Hello Gemma listen….I know I shouldn't call… but I think I've left my wallet somewhere in the bedroom… I can't find it anywhere…Please, please can you look for it and give me a bell on my mobile…..see you Friday if Danny is out…love you….bye!"

I fall into my comfortable chair and await the feeling of remorse - which doesn't come.

Absurd.

Paul McMahon – Dead Reckoning

Night No.1-Exsoteric disciple:

I skulk around in the black and pause to attend a seminar on the other side of 2-22, about the business model employed by a successful dealer called 'Tigger'. I am impressed with his ability to communicate whist clearly three sheets to the wind. He is explaining to a younger prisoner how to maximise the return off "his investment" by altering the purity of his stock. He has his props laid out before him and maintains eye contact with the mark whist he goes about his demonstration. He holds aloft a paracetamol tablet in his left hand and a small wrap in his right, like a proud market trader.

Tigger: I present to you in my right hand diacetylmorphine - heroin, smack, skag, brown, shit, dirt, gear, cheese, tar; and in my left : paracetamol, otherwise known... as 'bash'. This is a generic name for the adulterants that are mixed with H by us unscrupulous dealers, to maximise the volume of the deal, usually one part bash for two parts smack. Bash has the same properties as brown in that it runs across the foil in the same way when chasing the dragon, right?

Tigger produces a lighter from somewhere, like a magician, and the younger man is suitably impressed. 'Tigger', picks up prop two, a piece of foil, and continues his performance.

Paul McMahon – Dead Reckoning

Tigger: The tablets are crushed into a fine powder right, and heated on foil - 'ence.

Tigger sparks the lighter using a needlessly flashy manoeuvre, and runs his open palm slowly across the foil to display it, as if he where appearing in an advert.

Tigger: The powder begins to melt and then the foil is tilted. The oil that runs off the powder quickly congeals, discoloured, and hardens.

His voice changes and I can sense the finale' is approaching…

Tigger*:* This is then crushed again, and, BINGO, it is now virtually indistinguishable from real heroin in every way, thus bulking up its volume and bulking up your pocket, sunshine.

I have to sit on the urge to clap; I've heard the speech before many times, as Tigger screens his cell mates as prospective investors, but still, a good version tonight.

Night No.2 - Lessons from behind the fourth wall:

I climb the steps onto the 3s skilfully avoiding the old creaky hot spots that act as look out for the crafty con. I stop as my head breaks level with the next landing floor and peer under the cracks in the nearest doors, noting who is - and who is not - in light. This done, I creep up onto the landing, slowly approach 3-18 and come to rest against the wall outside.

Robinson is a middle aged, bald, white, fat, selective dyslexic. He can't read any instructions, or prison orders, but doesn't require any assistance ordering from the prison canteen sheets, filling in request complaint forms against myself or Gav, or studying horses' form in the papers. His cell mate is reading a letter aloud for him:

"...and for that I am truly sorry. I never meant to hurt you my love. Ohh Phone that fella and tell him I've left something at your gaff please honey. The last few days before I got lifted by the filth were great. You got to understand that I don't want to be with her but I have to stand by the kids, 'cos I'm a good man. Thanks for sending the PlayStation Debby, and I promise we will be together one day. Can you send me in £20 for some toothpaste? I love you girl. David."

Cell Mate: Don't you think you should end it with a kiss or something? I mean does she have a name that she calls you, like...Snuggles or something?"

Robinson: Nahh...fuck it, that'll do. As long as she sends me a 'score' its cushdy mate...yeah that looks proper... you got real neat writing, cheers mate. Nice job...this one finks I've been to uni and everyfink, silly old tart, I'll post vem two off togever tomorra', the uver ones my missus' birfday card, better late than never eh?

I saw Robinsons wife on a visit last year; a woman living in a parallel universe, oblivious to her husband's bad character in our realm. She spent the whole slot, head tilted, sympathetically nodding at his rantings about the injustice of it all, and our infringements of his human rights. I wonder if even he takes himself seriously. She is a woman in need of a great shake awake, so I scrawl the words "post" in my pocket book to remind me to swap his envelopes over when I empty the post box tomorrow night. That should do it. Sure his wife will like to get that letter instead.

Night No.3 - Baccus works in mysterious ways:

I fall down the last twelve steps in the dark. Limping into the office on the 1s, I sit down in the Talbot recliner to inspect my newly swollen wrist. Some fool, who clearly doesn't understand it, has adjusted the settings. I spend as long as I can resetting it one handed, and look at the clock, disappointed that only four minutes have passed. These are long shifts, these night shifts. The next few hours I shall have to fill constructively on my own, to avoid falling asleep. For inspiration I gaze around the office at sealed evidence bags on the floor, half competed paperwork, out of date inmate recall appeal packs down the side of cabinets, and home made weapons scattered on the desk. Disgraceful. I decide to start with the S/O's desk, sorting the papers into the only categories I can apply: 'too late to do', and 'almost too late to do'. The home made weapons I place in the sharps box, and the rest I push off into a black bin liner. Looking good. I stop momentarily to survey my work and notice a hissing sound coming from the bin liner. I decide it is far-fetched to worry if there may be a snake inside, no matter how tired I am.

A quick search reveals a container with a microscopic hole in its lid, containing a urine-coloured liquid from which a smell is emanating - a strong, familiar smell. I unscrew the lid to a now loud, hissing sound, as the grateful plastic relaxes and the fermented gas makes a break for it. I peer inside and see floating bits of banana, apple and bread. I also spot what looks like a Jacob's cracker, and can smell what I assume was once apple juice. Some inmate has taken great care in the production of this, for it is

Paul McMahon – Dead Reckoning

rather a good hooch, and well-disguised. I hold it up to the strip lights at 35 degrees and note its heavy rim against the plastic, its madeirised colour and, after a swirl to aerate the brew and supercharge the atmosphere, its earthy, gamey nose. This is a well brewed, volatile hooch, with heavy legs. I raise the bottle to my lips and take a sip - for research purposes. The mouth is musty, it is heavy on the tongue, hot on the palate, and has a toasty finish. A well-rounded, balanced assault on the senses, and may have anaesthetic properties for my wrist. Think about something else.

What hits me now is the amount of defensive saliva my mouth has produced on impact with this vile stuff. It is either this or bile. I cannot decide, and very shortly after discarding the cup, nor have I the faculties to think about it further. My vision swims and my head fast-forwards to the pain stage without any dily-dallying around. It feels like I am on acid for the first few seconds, and then I am sick. What possesses people to drink this stuff I cannot comprehend - unless it is this rather enjoyable sense of confusion I am left with, and my own personal time zone. Quality. Vintage stuff. I take my time getting to the front desk.

My time.

It is quiet.

I am not feeling myself.

Paul McMahon – Dead Reckoning

I am not

feeling

much.

Veeeeeeeery quiet.

Noise forces you to concentrate solely on it.

To forsake your current

thought.

To betray your will.

Coerces you in an instant.

`   Demands distraction.

I suddenly realise that silence is the purest form of sound.

The early hours are deafening this way.

Forced into noting the kidnapping of time, and pray for its

release.

All attention on this one   sense.

Now I am sick a second time.

Paul McMahon – Dead Reckoning

I wake up in the 2s office with twenty minutes left of my shift. I have four of the five Suicide Watch books on the desk in front of me and I am sitting on the fifth. I can't recall anything else. As I haven't checked them all night I make up for it by selflessly sprinting to each of there doors, with no regard for my own personal headache. I then think about something else. All are okay. Well, all are alive. Well, all of them *look* alive. This is good enough. I am furious with myself, for my lack of due care and attention, and punish myself by writing lengthy hourly observations in each inmates booklet - where they should have been for last night - to the point where my wrist aches; this makes me feel better, last night's medicine having worn off. I then carefully retreat to the 1s, once again thanking a god I don't believe in for sparing me a death on my watch, and await the day staff.

Basic regime/Jetsam.

I have been deep in thought on the bus this morning. Things have not been going as planned of late. I have been distracted. I have taken my eye off the ball and have become undisciplined. My work has been suffering and that is not acceptable. I decide the time has come to alter my regime. I must be too comfortable. It is the only explanation. I have nothing to work for. Everybody must have an incentive. Maybe Kierkegaard was onto something. I slam the front door behind me and head straight for the sound system. I rip out the power cable, leads and the adjoining wires from the back, and stack it up on the floor, piece by piece. This done I scoop it up and march back to the front door, leaving the wires trailing behind me. The plug bounces in protest all the way down the fire escape. Arriving at Nick's front door, I kick my entry request and await his arrival. I can hear scuffling around under foot and see the ivy twitch in my peripheral vision. The furry little bastards really are settling in. It doesn't help that Nick seems to have dispensed with his dust bin and appears to have thrown his dinner direct from his door on to the garden floor. Fucking slob. The rats will dine well tonight; Royal Red Shrimp, a good choice. I underestimated him. I peer through the window and see Nick is asleep on the couch at the back of the flat. Again. Committed to the idea, I toss the stereo into the nearest bin and begin to climb the steps again. Back to the top. Twelve steps.

Zones:

I gather up the now dusty magazines from behind the front door as a reward for my new found dedication, and take them into the front room. I begin to scour the pages for my coastal paradise. It is a big, long-term plan, this move. I have to be ready for when I get out of the job, whenever that may be. I find a few articles about the history of the area, the house prices, and the night life. I cut out the relevant ones and take each to the appropriate wall of my flat; the flat is sectioned off so as not to be confusing. I use my adhesive stick and glue each one up, making sure each join is clean and there is no overlapping. Some pages have been covered up as my idea changes or the sailing school/bakery, etc. closes and the article becomes obsolete, but for the most part if it goes up it stays up. I spend as much time here as I can. I sit in my chair, and shut my eyes, and drift off.

Night No.4 - Quarantine:

There is shouting coming from the 2s somewhere. I leave it long enough for the problem to sort itsself out and then take the obligatory walk upstairs. As I start across the 1s landing I notice a noise from the gated cell to my right. This type of cell has no door, merely a gate, so as to enable the officer to see all around the cell and not have to open the door to supply food and water. This wing has one such space, and it is rarely used. On inspection I find the occupant, a young black man, sitting on the bed with a length of bed sheet in his hands which he is fashioning into a ligature. I look around the cell and see there is nothing else to hand apart from a carton of mango juice near the gate at the front of the cell. He is naked apart from a non-rip, flame-retardant blanket at the foot of the bed; standard issue for disturbed prisoners. The young black lad is talking to himself. I look up at the top of the cell window and see the tail-end of some light green material flapping in the breeze. It appears the black lad has ripped someone's line hanging down from the window above - some wise cons use to refrigerate their drinks, or more commonly to pass drugs from one cell window to another. On this occasion it seems the black lad has had quite enough of whatever it is he has taken and doesn't want the mango juice either. The inmate above the black lad is screaming about his juice and threatening to kill whoever it is who had the balls to steal "from a bad boy". I glance at the cell card outside the gated cell. A6009CT is displayed, but no name on it. It is always harder to get someone's attention when calling them 'mate'; I experiment with an alternative:

Me: Alright bud?

A6009CT continues to entwine the green strips into a noose and ramble onto himself about showing them he means "what he says". A non-starter. I observe him look around the cell for a ligature point to attach the sheets to, knowing in this special 'anti ligature cell' there are only two places he could accomplish this. A6009CT impresses me and finds one. I get his attention by rattling the gate. He freezes like a deer. Standoff. I prepare my soft voice, and deliver my opening gambit:

Paul McMahon – Dead Reckoning

Actual conversation No. 6:

Me: Here… that knot's never gonna' hold your weight, buddy. Give it me tie the noose properly for you

Deer: No

Me: Honestly. You've tied what amounts to a reef knot, mate, it can't be trusted - it slips and comes undone. I'll tie you a poacher's knot, or the Gallows knot if you want, but I wouldn't recommend them as they kill by strangulation. If it's a snapped neck you're after then I'll do you an authentic hangman's noose knot, its more merciful see?

      A6009CT unhooks the sheet and wobbles over to the gate. As he gets nearer I see his pupils have dilated completely. He has stale white phlegm in both corners of his mouth like a rabid hyena, smells of sick, is totally incoherent, and is sweating like a paedophile in a playground. There must be some bad gear around, I think. I'm disappointed he wasn't more sport really, that was like taking candy from a baby. There is no reply. 'Rabies' will not remember this in the morning I am sure, and won't believe me if I choose to tell him. Poor lad. I fetch my Talbot recliner out the office and sit and watch him for a while. He is not on constant supervision but it is good for one's resolve to look upon what one can become when one loses one's grip. There is nothing on the TV for another twenty minutes, and I have checked the self-harmers. I estimate that if I'm lucky, I might just be in time for the panic attack. Rabies looks as if he is coming down from his hit. All that awaits him now is the long drop. The crash. I begin to resent Rabies as I concede he is to disappoint me a second time, at which point he scares himself by touching his face without realising it. In such a state it is the only nudge he needs, and he yelps in a big

Paul McMahon – Dead Reckoning

breath. This in turn sets off a pacey hyperventilation, which has the effect of making him burst into tears. He is in the zone, finding fear in everything. Choking on his tears, Rabies retches, clutches at his chest and, trembling, finally curls up in the foetal position. Bravo! That was worth waiting for. Crack. *Definitely* Crack. If only this were a game show; 'Guess the gear', I would be in the money now. I move the carton out from the front of the cell in case he comes up with an ingenious way of harming himself with fruit juice, and return my Talbot recliner to the office.

Night No.5 - Stemming the Tide:

It is 4am and I am at my low trough. My eyes feel alien to my head and aren't actually speaking to my brain any longer. It is a constant to and fro-ing between states. An emergency cell bell is illuminated and I rise up out of the Talbot reluctantly. It's coming from the 1s, so not far to walk and I can hear what the argument is before I arrive at the cell. I open the flap and politely ask their age, inform them of the time, and then settle it by telling them if they can't share the remote control then the TV goes off. With that I flick the in-cell electric off at the isolator box outside the door and saunter back to the Talbot. I answer the bell twice more. They take two very different approaches to get the power back on, neither of which wash with me. Consistency is paramount here.

I'm now sat back along the landing and am convinced I'm hallucinating, visualising water seeping out of the cell. As it turns out this is attempt number three to get me to change my mind. Novices. This one is always good for a laugh. It's common practise to flood a cell, and in turn a wing, when confined, to cause the staff as much of a 'problem' as possible. This is usually attempted by new inmates who have a flash of inspiration and are convinced this is a foolproof original idea. I decide to employ my favourite counter attack:

Paul McMahon – Dead Reckoning

1.   Select a few dirty blankets from the laundry sack.
2.   Soak them each in water.
3.   Roll them into sausages.
4.   Arrange in parallel lines, constructing river banks from the problem cell....
5.   ...to any hard bastard on the landing's cell.

The tide is dictated and the landings usual draining mechanisms are negated. The trick is then to ensure the flaps are closed on the landing and simply walk away. After a couple of minutes the nominated ally realises and loses his cool, and I can hear him screaming out the cell to whoever is listening to stop the "Fucking flood". No sooner than it has started the flow dries up. I will have managed to book both trouble makers a slap without having to get my hands dirty. I have ended the shift on a high. All present and correct, Sir. I can do this.

Less is more:

The bus journey home goes without a hitch. The driver is courteous, my seat is vacant on the top deck and the traffic is all going the other way. I set my stop watch as we pull off and tell myself that this could be the record breaker. It falls a little short.

Paul McMahon – Dead Reckoning

I walk naked into my living room, having de-robed in the hall. I stop and stare long and hard at the CD cabinet, awaiting inspiration, before pulling Chet Baker out of his haze. It is not until I have spent a minute or so trying to work out what sort of thief would break into a scabby flat, in a non-affluent area, and steal nothing but a battered 1980s Pioneer stereo (missing the rewind button), that I remember leaving it downstairs for Nick.

No time like the present:

Without giving the idea much thought, save for that it would "only take a second", I find myself running down the fire escape to the garden as naked as the day I was born, bar a few pubes, flapping about freely. I arrive outside Nick's door and can see my stereo just as I'd left it at the bottom of Nicks bin. Thank God for that. I bend down to pick it up and scoop it into my arms. It is a little wet from the dew, and I have to momentarily adjust my grip. This caesura is my downfall. It is fortunate for the stereo that I am not of a nervous disposition; when I hear a loud scream from directly behind me, generated by Nick as he opens his door to the sight of a pimply, hairy arse hole winking at him, I'm able to avoid dropping it. He has slammed his door again by the time I turn around to explain, not that I would have been able to improvise an appropriate apology in sufficient time worthy of soothing Nicks state of mind after such a horrific experience. Maybe I could tell him it was a joke, or maybe deny all knowledge of what just happened, as he may not have recognised my arse. Either way, the arse is cold, and this will have to wait.

Paul McMahon – Dead Reckoning

Karmic residue:

Once back in the warm and reconnected, I press play and skip through most of the album until I come to "The Thrill Is Gone". I love this particular recording. I go into the kitchen to retrieve a tumbler, knowing I have exactly 64 seconds to get comfy in my chair before old Chet starts singing. He comes in perfectly, just in time, just like he does every time. I raise my glass on *that* line, just like always, and listen for every slip, every glorious error he makes through this perfect song. I am in good spirits; the answer machine is no match for me now. I do a little quick step, shuffle over to it and flick play:

Answerphone Man: Who the Fuck is this? If I ever find out who you are I'm gonna kill you...do you understand? I swear to God I'm going to fucking kill you...

There is a loud banging noise, and the speaker cone of my answer machine almost jumps out of its socket trying to accommodate its ferocity, followed by some more shouting, this time further away, doubtlessly the same voice but too distant to make out any words. I can now hear some different shouting but in another key, at least a few octaves up, presumably a woman's, or a very high baritone. She clearly has had no vocal training; her breath is not supported and her voice breaks as she pushes for a crescendo on the lyric "he-lp". The woman is wailing in the wrong time signature. Unwilling to let her spoil Chet, I turn him up. Her screams become lost in the music as Chet begins his Trumpet solo at 98 seconds. The message has finished by the time the song has faded out and my bourbon is gone. I reasonably conclude the mystery lady must be Gemma. Karma has run its course and she

Paul McMahon – Dead Reckoning

has received her dose. I wish I could tell Michelle. I toy with the idea that her number must be almost identical to mine, hence Gemma's original error, so it is just possible I could guess it. I feel so righteous now. I walk over to the CD cabinet and pour myself a large whiskey as a reward. I deserve this one, I really do. Poor bitch.

Night No.6 - Nothing to report

It is 03:31hrs. There has not been one solitary cell bell for the last hour. It seems they have all got the message that I am on duty this week and there isn't much point trying your luck. In the absence of any stimulation I find myself pondering the big stuff.

1)   I don't think I would recognise the back of my hand in a line up.

2)   I wouldn't let these fuckers out if they can't read. Fuck everything else. The sentence plans, rehab programmes, psychology, fuck it all. It's all bollocks. You're going nowhere pal if you can't read. Theft? Life sentence till you can read a fucking sentence. Simple.

Happiness is door-shaped:

It is 03:32hrs, there is absolutely nothing to do. All the prisoners are locked behind their doors in the Land of Nod or covertly bashing the bishop, and there is not a soul to be seen anywhere on the Wing. Even the cockroaches have turned in for the night. This is blissful. This was blissful. I'm now actually bored. So bored I amble up to the landings to be nosy in the dark, in search of a problem to occupy myself. There is the usual smell of weed wafting out the cells. There is so much marijuana on the wing that going up to the 3's actually makes me cough a little. It stinks. Quite a nice stink, but a stink nonetheless. I spend a long time sniffing at the cell doors purely in order to make a list of the cells to target in the morning for piss tests and cell searches - if the day staff have the time. I take a few deep breaths from some doors to ascertain whether it is in fact weed or a joss stick. There are lots and lots of cells, so they probably won't have time, but I do it anyway as I am really bored. The lads are really blazing it up hard and smoke is billowing out of the T-boy's cell too. I leave him off the list though. I make the list up neatly and finish writing up a long Security Information Report on the front desk, which I then attach it to. This done I have a little hunger pang feeling, a distinct yearning for a chocolate bar, so I eat my Snickers. Then I crack open my bag of Minstrels. The bag makes me laugh a little bit. It's a funny bag. Now I've finished my sweets, I sit down again with nothing to do. I begin to ruminate. To ponder. This silence is making me think a lot.

Philosophy of punishment:

I feel tonight that I am a tool for retribution, a cog in the social contract machinery that operates between offender and society. A physical manifestation of punishment, calibrated through training to produce deterrence in a rational conservative paradigm, and imbued with the responsibility to ensure proportionality of retribution in order to redress the imbalance of the victim. I realise the importance of being a balanced and impersonal tool in this vast process, to negate the need for the victim's individual revenge, which would be personal and vindictive; and so *I* really am a necessary *good*.

Paul McMahon – Dead Reckoning

However the revolving door of offenders into custody which pops into my mind from leftfield, presents me with a philosophical problem. The punishment can only be said to be positive if there is a greater good, or a benefit to the community which orders its delivery. I suddenly feel a deep profound fear that the punishment does not deter. I am consumed by anxiety at the thought that there is no benefit when the criminal is not rehabilitated and therefore punishment serves no purpose, meaning its continued delivery after this realisation is nothing more than societal revenge masquerading as retribution, and I am involved in this conspiracy - and so *I* really am an unnecessary *evil*.

I become a little emotional when I think how those great minds before me have had to bear the cross of being midwives to men's thoughts their entire lives. My mental wrangling unfolds itself into fully blown paranoia when I realise that Oscar 1 might be coming round to check my paperwork, so I check my paperwork over and over again. Then I start looking for a Kit-Kat.

Night No.7 - Threatening behaviour:

There is a cell bell coming from the 2s landing at 01:13hrs. I wander up with my sandwich as I don't intend on being there long. As I reach the end of the stairs I can hear raised voices. One voice is shouting about somebody being a nonce. The other voice is taking exception to this. There are other voices shouting as well but fainter, as if they are shouting out the windows, which is exactly what they *are* doing, encouraging *somebody* to give somebody *else* a going over.

Paul McMahon – Dead Reckoning

I slam open the observation flap of the cell door from which the argument is coming from to announce my arrival. However the sound of the observation flap slamming back on its hinges against their metal door doesn't have the desired effect of alerting the occupants to my presence. They are so caught up in insulting each other that they pay me no notice. I don't like being ignored. I would like to open the door and give them a damn good kicking, but I can't. On nights we do not have keys. They are taken off me when I report for duty. I am instead issued with a sealed pouch, inside which is a cell key. I am only to break into this pouch in an emergency or else face disciplinary action. I have never broken in to the pouch. 'Emergency' is so subjective.

Pouch Politics:

1)   I am ordered that I should *never* go into a cell at night alone.
2)   Oscar 1 carries cell keys at night, and it is only they that respond to an emergency.

In conclusion - If I am not to go into a cell (without Oscar 1, who has keys anyway) then *why* have I any need for a sealed cell key pouch at all? I find that I do NOT have any need for the pouch. Besides, the paperwork involved with breaking into the pouch is horrendous - so I hear. I have tried to refuse the pouch several times before on this principle when I've attended duty, but I am given some drivel about 'duty of care', and the need to 'preserve life'. Apparently preservation of life supersedes security, and I have the sealed pouch forced upon me anyway for this spurious reason. You can take a horse to water but you can't make it drink.

Paul McMahon – Dead Reckoning

The two lads have evidently found some reason not to want to remain in each other's company a second longer, which is unfortunate seeing as how it's not very easy to get away from somebody when you're both locked in a cell. The more shouty one of the two, with a higher pitched voice, tells me in a tone that people usually only use to threaten people, that they are going to have a fight unless I move one of them. I explain to the 'shouter' that a key ingredient of a threat, if not the whole point of it, is that the consequence you are promising must have an adverse effect on the person that you are trying to threaten, or else is not really a threat at all. Therefore, because it isn't me he is 'threatening' to fight, this entire disagreement is completely inconsequential to me and so, after taking a bite of my sandwich, I bid them both goodnight.

As if in an attempt to test my theory, the less shouty one with a lower pitched voice punches the other one in the back of the head before I can shut the flap. Not very hard. It is the sort of punch that says, "I don't really want to hit you, and I don't really want you to hit me back so I'm just going to do it hard enough that it can't be mistaken as a 'stroke' or 'hair ruffle'. Higher Pitch obviously hasn't picked up on the subtle nuances of the 'punch'; he delivers a blow back, so lightning quick and with so much force that it puts Lower Pitch down in the chair at the back of the cell. Higher Pitch looks round at me with a self-satisfied look that says "I told you so, how stupid do you feel now", just in time to see me taking a bite out of my sandwich. I have my mouth full and, not wanting to be rude, chew my food a few times and swallow it before I speak.

Paul McMahon – Dead Reckoning

Actual conversation No. 7:

Me: Please, don't mind me, carry on. Its cheese and tomato by the way, on wholemeal, in case you're wondering.

Higher P: What the fuck is wrong with you, you Psycho?

Me: I'm hungry.

Lower P: Are you fucking serious!?

Higher P: Shut up! I swear to God, I'm gonna' fucking kill him if you don't get him out of my cell.

Me: Firstly, I take my diet very seriously on night shifts; they alter your body's natural circadian rhythm. Secondly, it's not your cell, it's the Queen's, and thirdly…no I don't have a thirdly, just get on with it.

Higher P: GET HIM OUT!

Lower P: Please get me out of here Gov.

Higher P: Thank you! You see, he wants out.

Me: Thank you? Very civil, congratulations, you're getting on better already. Goodnight gents.

I slam the flap and walk off munching on my sandwich. I can hear a few more noises that sound like they could be punches. They could also be the sound which accompanies star jumps, squats, and other components of a cell work out. It's an easy mistake to make. Think about something else.

Paul McMahon – Dead Reckoning

Jump the Yardarm:

I arrive back at the flat in good time, and have a large glass of Rioja before crawling into bed with a bottle of gin. What is to follow now is a strictly necessary, tried and tested method of readjusting the shift-lag. This method is so successful that is not just employed by seasoned drinkers. I can provide the names of three colleagues that drink only on a weekend, and one that drinks only at Christmas, that have subscribed to my method due to its unqualified success. As tired as I am now at 08:10hrs in the morning having worked all night, if I get drunk now, and I mean really wrecked enough, it is possible to sleep through the remainder of the day, and the night, and awake this time tomorrow morning fresh as a daisy, having shaken off my nocturnal existence in one single, ultra-long sleeping session. An internal clock reversal in 24 hours. It is genius and it works. No need to think about anything else.

Zzzzzzzzzzzzzzzzzzz

I spy with my little eye:

I don't know which me has woken up this morning; no doubt time will tell. I have slept in until 07:15hrs, meaning almost a full solid day of unconsciousness. Other than a bit of a headache I feel fine, a good effort. I have a week now without work. This was designed by the system to give my body the chance to reset itself by daylight hours.; very thoughtful of them, the by-product of litigation no doubt. The sounds outside are rare to me and I am unable to sleep because of them. I also realise that I haven't got a curtain in this room, and that I have never been here at this time in the daylight for it to bother me before. It is also too hot; I would usually have left hours ago and the boiler is still kicking in to heat a normally empty flat. I do some mental arithmetic and conclude I could knock about £90 a year off my gas bill if I were to remedy this oversight. I turn over in bed and shuffle around until I have found a position I think is more conducive to sleep, not that I need it. I lie here on my front for a while looking at the carpet, trying to decide what colour it started its boring life as. I decide it probably used to be light beige. If I was pressed further I would say egg shell. I begin to plan my itinerary for the day, seeking out Nick, getting 'de-prioritised' as I go. I am procrastinating. This lie-in business is severely overrated. Besides, I know full well my headache will get no better without two litres of water. Unhelpfully there is no tap in here. The architect of this flat was certainly not a pisshead.

Needs must:

Drinking straight from the mains in the kitchen, I eventually concede I shall have to make my peace with Nick as he is the only person I know in this street. He is also the only person I know 'personally' in this borough - apart from the talkative young girl who works in the off licence round the corner and whose name escapes me. I wander into the hallway and root around in the

Paul McMahon – Dead Reckoning

washing bin for some clothes. I've really let the place go lately, more than normal. I shuffle a few sausages out of the way and pull out a handful of non-uniform clothes. There is a roll neck jumper at the bottom which I reckon has another wear left in it, so I grab hold of the sausage on top of it to get it out the way. As I do so I can feel a little inconsistency in the material skin. Intrigued by its contents I slip a hand inside and rummage around the innards. I lay a hand on a bent bit of card in the trouser arse pocket, and pull it out to inspect. I recognise the card immediately as the little logo is splashed up all around at work for the Cons, and allow myself a chuckle as I now understand why 'Landlubber' was so good to me. The card is a business type flyer card for AA. I make a promise to myself to attend. Just to attend. Just once. I would do it today but I have a bridge that needs repairing.

I meander downstairs after dressing as much of me as is possible, having put on the roll neck jumper and thick long trousers in recompense for yesterday evening's exposé. I tap on the door at a volume and tempo very much consistent with that of a repentant neighbour.

The door opens. Nick is 5' 5", has very short black hair, and is a Japanese/ Italian mix. He has on thick framed NHS glasses, perched on a bruised nose, heavy stubble, and is wearing a crusty blue towelling dressing gown. It is approximately 09:34hrs.

I have been standing here for at least ten seconds. The bastard's not going to make this easy for me.

Actual conversation No. 8:

Me: Er…about last night Nick. I was in a rush. Sorry mate.

Nick: What were you doing?

Me: I came to get my stereo out your bin?

Me: Of course you did. Look, I've seen you in some states right? But when it becomes un-neighbourly, you've got to rein it in - we've all got problems.

Least said, soonest mended:

I sense a quick decision is needed here, so I tell him I'm "sorry".

Blah, blah, blah:

There is a beat, so I ad lib with an assertion that it won't happen again, and that I'm taking steps to address my problem(s). Nick seems content with this and, being neighbourly, invites me into his flat.

A friend in need:

Nick is looking dishevelled, more so than usual. I enquire about his job as a conversation starter, whilst looking for his Absinth. As soon as the last syllable leaves my lips I wish above all else I could catch its coat tails and swallow it back up. Two tear drops simultaneously roll from each eye at terminal velocity down Nick's cheeks, like they had been waiting in the wings, raring their invisible microscopic motorbikes for their cue. This is followed by an unwordly squeal, the sort achievable by the voice box only when air is sucked in past it the wrong way. There is a brief pause here now between inhale and exhale in which I consider running

Paul McMahon – Dead Reckoning

for the door. Realising I won't make it, I prepare myself for the imminent wailing, the sobbing, the bloody screaming, the boo-hoo-hoo-ing and the God-why me-ing. I am understandably relieved then when Nick simply sputters, and slumps into his knees on the sofa. Silent.

Thank Fuck for that. He is all cried out. Marvellous. I am not in the mood to have to 'back pat' and spout optimistic maxims for the rest of the evening. I give him a minute or so of alone time to gather himself and come to terms with being unemployed again whilst I look for the sugar cubes and the tea strainer. I'm certain he doesn't want anyone mollycoddling him at the moment; I'm sure after all, it's not his culture. Whatever that is.

As I finish arranging the equipment on the tray I decide I ought to check Nick, as he hasn't moved for a few minutes. He's quite hard to wake so I slap him; he must have worn himself out with his weeping. I sit Nick up in the sofa and he comes round enough to tell me that I have always been a good friend to him. Stress and high emotion can really make people very sentimental; I don't ever remember doing anything for Nick besides drinking and talking. I pour the Absinth over the sugar cube in the tea strainer onto the cracked ice, and watch it turn a luminescent green. This done I pass Nick his glass and I propose a toast, "To new beginnings". Nick drinks his down in one and lets his eyes close, exhausted.

I should really be here when he wakes up, in case he wants to talk it over, plan his next move, so I retrieve some more ice from the galley part of the studio and crush it in a tea towel, returning back to the sofa to prepare two more drinks. This done, I swap Nick's empty glass for a replenished one and slip it into his hand so it is balancing on his stomach, propped up by the knot in his dressing gown. I drink mine. My head is swimming with wormwood now, so I dispense with the ice and pour myself an extra large measure in case I don't have time to prepare it as normal. This stuff really sprints up on you.

Zzzzzzzzz...Zzzzzzzzzzzzzzzzzzzzzzzzz...Z..Z..Zzzzzz (Part 1)

My phone's ringing wakes me up at 2:02hrs, which it couldn't help really, considering I have fallen asleep on the floor of my flat a tongue's reach from it. It's a bittersweet position in truth, as although the ear-splitting ringing is as relaxing as a Taser, my body's proximity means I don't have to put any effort into answering it. I knock the handset off the base unit with a sluggish finger and pull the receiver under my head, inventing a dual purpose communication pillow. In preparation to communicate, I clear my throat into the receiver. This noise acts as the starting pistol for a verbal eruption to explode out of the blocks with ultrasonic speed:

Voice: ThereisahostagesituationonAwingandnoneofthenegotiators areavailablecanyougettherenow?"

Me: urrrrgh? (1)

Grunt semantics:

Grunt (grŭnt)

v. **grunt·ed, grunt·ing, grunts**

v.intr.

Paul McMahon – Dead Reckoning

1. To utter a deep guttural sound, as a hog does.

2. To utter a sound similar to a grunt, as in disgust.

v.tr.

To utter or express with a deep guttural sound: *He merely grunted his (dis)approval.*

(1)   This particular grunt is a drowsy, confused grunt which goes up tonally at the end, the sort of annoying upward tilt that Australians finish every sentence with, thus turning even a statement of fact regarding the presence of a sausage into a question (?). In conclusion, a grunt, YES, of this there can be no question, but a definite non-committal, puzzled sort of a grunt. What this grunt was NOT, was a "Yes, no problem, I'll be there in a jiffy" sort of a grunt. This, however, is evidently how it is misheard, being that the S/O hangs up before I can embark on any serious excuse making. Clever Bastard.

Zzzzzzzz…Zzzzzzzzzzzzzzzzzzzzzz…Z..Z..Zzzzzz (Part 2)

I am awoken a second time at 02:07hrs by the warning alarm a phone emits when it has been left off the hook too long. I jump up quickly up off the deck without consulting my body beforehand; a neat little trick I use to prevent any potential mutiny from unwilling sleepy limbs. I appreciate almost immediately, however that this tactic is better suited to leaving more luxurious terrains, such as double beds as opposed to bare floorboards. My right leg is now completely numb after enduring a night sandwiched against unyielding floorboards, meaning my rise is swiftly followed by my fall. Now floor level again, I use this opportunity to formulate a strategy to attend the incident. One that involves as little exertion as possible seems prudent considering my level of alertness and lack of sobriety, so I factor in yesterday's shirt and the Taxi firm opposite my flat into my strategic planning.

Shake a leg:

I approach the taxi firm opposite and surge through the tatty front door with real momentum. Time is of the essence and I make sure my entrance conveys the urgency of my journey. The only person to directly witness my appearance is an elderly black man who looks remarkably like an Ewok due to his attire. Ewok is wearing a warm looking duffle coat, hood up, drawstrings pulled round his little podgy face, sitting stock still next to a heater at the opposite end of the unit, peering out at me motionless behind what looks like rather unnecessary bullet-proof acrylic, even for South London.

I bound up to the counter, and as directed by the sign…

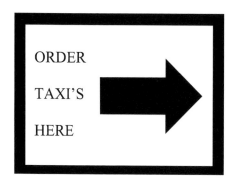

ORDER

TAXI'S

HERE

Paul McMahon – Dead Reckoning

…speak into the little voice grill next to it, directly in front of the Ewok, asking politely:

Me: Please may I have a TAXI?

The Little Ewok appears inconvenienced by my request for a taxi, which I find unjust considering my attempt at civility and all these visual prompts subconsciously encouraging me to do just that. Not to mention the fact we are in a taxi rank. After an incredulously long pause, during which I worry he might have died of disappointment, he eventually asks in a lazy Caribbean accent what time I want the cab for. It being ridiculously early in the morning, and there being no other conceivable reason for my standing here, I have to bite my tongue to stop myself stating the fucking obvious.

<u>The cut of his Jib:</u>

I change my mind about the bullet-proof acrylic. In light of our recent interaction, it is undeniably a proportionate security measure. After establishing that I would like the taxi *now*, he waves dismissively at me to sit down with his right elbow, without taking his hand out of his pocket. What a colossal Cunt. I would rather he honk up a clingy phlegm bullet and fire it in my face, than whisper through subtle physicality that I am not worthy of the most basic conventional norms of social interaction, and be deemed so beneath this discourteous dick that I am not even worth him lowering, even infinitesimally, the temperature of his hand.

Paul McMahon – Dead Reckoning

Two can play at this game.

The Spanish Bamboozle:

I recall a mind-fuck trick I learnt off a prisoner in Healthcare. In preparation I let my face relax to accentuate the contrast before suddenly assuming an expression of excited shock, like I have just recognised him from somewhere. I morph my expression into one of astonishment by gradually opening my mouth and widening my eyes, reinforced by the incorporation of a slow extending finger-point, as if realising something biblically important, and vocalise this with a

Me: Whoooooooooow!

Then I laugh naughtily and wag my finger at him, letting a broad cheeky grin grow knowingly across my face as if we are sharing a mischievous secret. Then I go to say something but stop quickly, flashing a glance round at two Somali chaps sat deep in conversation next to the door, shaking my head and miming that it's not safe to talk, before I turn and start to leave. At this point I throw in my best 'Columbo' impression, spinning back towards him, momentarily primed to say "One more thing", but stop at the formulation of the first consonant as if thinking better of it. I pause for drama. Seeing the business cards on the desk I pick one up, slip it into my inside breast coat pocket and pat it sneakily. I then mime a phone shape with my outstretched finger and thumb, wink theatrically and nod my head at him. This done I turn around and saunter toward the chair, shaking my head in mock disbelief and

Paul McMahon – Dead Reckoning

giggling at something utterly hilarious, leaving the Ewok with a stunned look of bewilderment on his boat race.

I have absolutely no idea what any of that was about, but it must have fucked with his head. Think about something else.

Time and Tide waitith for no man:

The two Somali pirates briefly look up at me approaching the one remaining seat between them that I have been elbow-ushered to sit in. I pause to allow time for one of them to move. Nothing happens. We are in a manners black hole. I nestle myself clumsily in between them. They continue their conversation in their mother tongue, unperturbed, as if I am not there. This annoys me slightly, as I have no idea what they're saying and I am most likely an authority on the subject. To my mind Ewok has made no obvious attempt to assist me in the act of procuring a car, despite his being the precise business that the sign outside purports him to be in, and presumably his only function in the entire operation. Under my careful scrutiny I know categorically that he has only pressed his little microphone thingy once since my arrival, and from what I can decipher, unless one of the taxi's call signs is "CURRY GOAT 1", there is no taxi arranging happening whatsoever.

Four minutes go by on the battered clock without so much as an apology or an estimated time of arrival. I am eyeballing the still baffled Ewok in his little bubble, when the two Somali chaps stand up and hug each other farewell over my head; both their crotches brush my ears. The one to my right leaves and the

Paul McMahon – Dead Reckoning

remaining Pirate looks down at me and says in a brand spanking new East-End accent "Alright Geez, where are we going".

I would do a life sentence for this prick here and now, but I make do with a glare and reply dryly "Prison". I even drop the please. That'll learn the Cockney bastard. Think about something else.

Better late than never:

I am deposited outside the front gate by my cabbie and am ushered through the staff lock by expectant staff who look like they are lining the home straight of a track event, before I can pay the fucker. Distracted/drunken/ly I throw my key tallies at the key chute, which predictably miss and bounce on the floor. One of the spectators hurriedly gathers them up on my behalf, needlessly however, as I find my keys are already in the outstretched hand of Oscar 1, who is standing at the last gate waving his arm onwards and shooing me along out the gate lodge toward the wing like a personal trainer. I stubbornly amble through but he breaks into a canter in front, forcing me into a light jog to keep up, all the while reeling off times and names at me, none of which I can remember as I am still preoccupied by thoughts of the befuddled Ewok. I arrive at the main building to find staff with pips on their shoulders crammed into every inch of the passageway, talking at speed. I hold my breath on the way past out of respect. Upon arrival at the finish line I am greeted with an uninspiring roll of the eyes by my S/O, who points at the 2s landing and gestures to get on with it.

Paul McMahon – Dead Reckoning

Actual Conversation No 9 Part 1:

Staff member: I understand that you must feel frustrated about the situation, It's clear you think you've been hard done by.

Voice: Fuck off.

Staff member: I'm sorry that I'm upsetting you; It's not my intention to…

Voice: Are you deaf? FUCK OFF or he dies right now.

I wobble up to the landing making a lot of very un-strategic noise bouncing along the railings, the sound of which notifies the poor member of untrained staff who stumbled across this mess of my arrival; they literally burst into tears of relief at the sight of me and run off without so much as a by-your-leave. I find myself suddenly the sole occupant of the landing and reluctantly advance to the cell door of 2-22, behind which the hostage situation is taking place, without much time to un-drink my thoughts. Whilst I'm concentrating on standing as still as my drunkenness permits my key chain clatters against the metal, announcing that there is most definitely somebody here. A voice shouts through the locked cell door-

Actual Conversation No. 9 Part 2:

Gobby: I JUST told you to FUCK OFF! I don't want to speak to anyone…if you don't fuck off right now I'm going to cut his throat…do you hear?

Paul McMahon – Dead Reckoning

Me: Who the fuck do you think you're talking to???

Gobby: Eh?

Me: Do you think I want to be standing here Gobby? Eh? I haven't dragged my fucking arse in here at 3am, to stand here listening to you talk to me like some kind a' cunt!

'Gobby' does not reply immediately to this, probably out of shock. I don't add anything for the moment either. Definitely due to shock. The only audible reaction in fact is from down stairs, that of group gasping and the sound of collective foreheads being rubbed. I imagine there is some discussion about rule books and defined strategy, but I have never been able to guarantee engaging my brain before my mouth. I'll explain later that it's just prison banter, an attempt to establish a rapport of some description. I must I have been called for a reason, and it might just be that someone values my fresh take on interpersonal skills. There is no point changing how I interact with the fuckers now. Think about something else. I'm going to get on a level with this bastard. We are the same, me and him. I'll find a way in. It shouldn't be too hard. Booze breeds confidence in me; I have a captive audience and feel like a movie star.

Actual Conversation No.9 Part 3:

Gobby: Who the fuck are you???

Me: Listen… they're gonna make some cunt stand here whether you like it or not, so it might as well be someone half sensible, right?

Paul McMahon – Dead Reckoning

(Long Pause)

Me: Oi.

Gobby: Get me the Governor.

Me: The Governor? You're having a bubble. Even I can't get to see that fucker.

Gobby: Who are *you?*

Me: I'm a nobody. Foot soldier. Cannon fodder. No pips on me mate. I actually *work* in this shit hole. So what's the story anyway? No one tells me Jack Diddly...

Gobby: I shouldn't be here.

Me: Same here.

Gobby: No, I mean I'm not like the fucker in here, I'm only on remand, and I haven't done anything, I just had an argument with my missus...

Me: Women eh?

Gobby: She was fucking around on me...I just lost it. She's fine now, withdrawn the charges. I don't belong in this shit hole.

Me: So what's that got do with silly bollocks in there.

Paul McMahon – Dead Reckoning

Gobby: Nothing, I just need to get someone's attention, I'm supposed to be getting bail.

Me: Well I'm listening.

Gobby: You don't give a fuck.

Me: True…but I'm here aren't I…so you may as well spill your guts while you've got my attention.

Gobby: Who's out there with you?

Me: A couple of nosey bastards down the way, waiting for me to fuck up.

Gobby: Well fuck 'em off

Me: No probs. It'll be a pleasure…FUCK OFF!

Gobby: Are they gone?

Me: Sort off…hang about…you heard him; jog the fuck on.

Gobby: You're fucking different Gov.

Me: So they tell me.

Gobby: So what's the point of you here then?

Me: Don't get philosophical with me mate.

Gobby: Seriously, what happens now? What can you do for me?

Me: Nothing. I can only ask for you.

Paul McMahon – Dead Reckoning

Gobby: Ask for some fags.

Me: There's no point. They won't give 'em to you. Shout me to the door.

Gobby: Why?

Me: Just do it.

Gobby: COME TO THE DOOR!

I slip a Marlboro under the door, out of sight of the staff on the landing below, then return to my slouching position on the landing. The idea is to keep the perpetrator talking, but I know he must have been gagging for that cigarette, so I let him enjoy it. I have one too, simply to gauge the length of time. I let a while go by.

Me: What's your name?

Gobby: Danny.

Me: Danny…they're gonna be doing their nut downstairs worrying if he's still alright.

Danny: He's fine.

Me: Can I ask him if he's ok?

Danny: No. you speak to me.

Me: Well can you ask him if he's ok?

Paul McMahon – Dead Reckoning

Danny: You alright? (grunt) He's fine.

Me: Cheers…so this bird? She your other half, eh?

Danny: Gemma?

Wind out the sails:

My fantasy implodes. My eyes open wide, and I instantly need to urinate as my bladder contracts. Surely not. There are at least 7,172,091 people in London according to this year's POA branch pub quiz. There is a silence which I can't bring myself to fill. Silence is not good in a hostage situation. Eventually I ask Danny what happened.

I already know what happened and I don't want to hear it. Why ask questions when we don't like answers?

Spin the yarn:

Danny begins to tell me how he has come home after a long day on site, and listened to this message on the answer machine from her bloke. He tells me how devastated he was. He tells me how, looking back, he always thought she had a fancy fella. He tells me they were having problems, but points out quite reasonably that most couples do. He tells me they have been married since they were both 18. His voice breaks a little as he describes her reaction when confronted, how she just denied it flatly, even in the face of indisputable evidence. Evidence he played

Paul McMahon – Dead Reckoning

over and over again. I'm no mathematician but the odds on our meeting must be lotteryesque. I slip in a subtle northern twang to my vowels, just to be on the safe side. He says that if she had just said sorry, shown a grain of remorse – anything - he wouldn't have *had* to do what he done, he could have "…swallowed it". He assures me they would have got through it but for her to lie through her teeth. It is unforgivable. I have to agree with him.

My usefulness as a negotiator has just expired. I am numb. I am taking up too much space. I can feel what I suspect very much may be a conscience. I have sobered up and realise the seriousness of the situation. I pull myself together by the age-old technique of coughing and pulling my trousers up. Done. There is another man in the cell after all. I run the occupants through my head. 2-22…2-22? It dawns on me that the victim is Robinson - For a change. At least he is a cunt. Thank God for small mercies.

Danny asks me if I have any more cigarettes, which I do but I want to save my last one for the taxi home. I tell Danny to have a look around the cell for cigarettes, as I know for a fact that Robinson smokes. After a while I hear Danny curse. He has found some tobacco but he can't roll up. I tell Danny that I can and offer to roll him one, as any good host would. At this point I can hear a muffled sound from Robinson, who must be gagged as it is impossible to understand what he is saying. Then I hear a thud; Danny must be reminding him who is in charge here, and it certainly isn't me. Danny slips the tobacco through the door and, after being granted permission by him, I collect it then go and lean back in my position on the railings.

Paul McMahon – Dead Reckoning

Serendipity:

Upon opening the packet I am greeted with the following:

1. Loose tobacoo
2. Wrap of heroin
3. Loose foils
4. Loose match sticks.

I'm about to share the oddity of the packet with Danny, but think better of it. I have seen first-hand the effects of heroin on a novice and decide this could be the 'Bruce-Willis' moment I have been waiting for. Cunningly I state:

Me: It's Old Holborn mate, not worth it; it'll taste like shit

Danny: I don't care what it is, just roll it; I'm roasting in here Gov.

Me: Ok bud.

This sort of decision really should be run past the bosses, but Buddha has betrayed me and I am not concerned with mortal managers tonight. I pull out a Rizla and coerce some tobacco into it. I then pull the wrap out and unravel it over the Rizla, toying with it, and fashion it into a roach like I have seen the cons do a million and one times before. The powdery contents fall directly into the middle of the Rizla. I insert my newly improvised filter into the end

Paul McMahon – Dead Reckoning

and begin the task of rolling the cigarette. This done, I raise the paper up to my lips in time for Danny to whisk away the obstruction from the observation glass.

Danny: Just checking Gov. You've been pretty quiet out there.

Me: I've only been blessed with one mouth, bud.

Athithophel:

I lick the Rizla and note how bitter the taste is. Once rolled, I put the spliff in between my lips and pull out my lighter. Adhering to smoking etiquette, I ask Danny if he minds me having the first puff. He does not object, like any good guest, and I light the cigarette. It crosses my mind that I may become affected by the heroin, may become a little light headed, but I assure myself it is for a good cause - and I have always wanted to try the forbidden fruit. Danny stands directly at the flap and watches me. I take a drag deep down for effect and sigh the smoke out slowly. I sow the seed by telling him it tastes a bit shitty, but remark that Old Holborn isn't premium tabacco. Danny, rather impatiently I feel, asks for the 'fag'. Put out, I slip the poison chalice under the door and stand back on the railings, with even less finesse than I had a minute ago. Clueless, Danny picks up the improvised sleeper and puts it to his mouth. He takes a drag and puffs on it.

Danny: You're right, it tastes like shit but it's better than nothing, eh?

Paul McMahon – Dead Reckoning

Splice the main brace:

I think to myself that the fire must now be near the 'skag', and hold my breath. Danny is contentedly smoking away and is none the wiser. After a couple of pulls I see the fag begins to give off a different sort of cloudy smoke, more stratocumulus than fractostratus, but luckily Danny is preoccupied and too problem-obsessed to notice. I pull my keys out of my pocket, which I should have been relieved of upon my arrival on the 1s. I pause briefly to ponder; if it goes the way of the pear, which manager's head will roll for this? Danny sits down on the bed and momentarily disappears from sight. I move closer to the door and silently shuffle my cell key to the front of the bunch. I wait for a sign. It comes in the form of Danny dropping the spliff on the floor and falling over stoned trying to pick it up. My key is in the door before I know it.

Danny is now lying face down on the floor, with a crooked smile on his face as the warm ball unfurls within him. I can hear the sound of heavy booted footsteps behind me on the stairs. Danny does not seem alarmed. I throw myself theatrically on top of him and shout, "No weapon, No weapon". It is the least I can do for him. Not that he will remember, fucking smackhead. Junk is a one-way street.

Skipper's Debrief:

I am in the latter stages of my dressing down, longing for my dressing gown. The Governor is running out of steam. He had begun well by covering my desertion of policy and my abandonment of my training, however the next part was unfocused

Paul McMahon – Dead Reckoning

and boring but I have tuned back in to listen to this, his current section concerning the disregard of my 'duty of care' to both 'residents'. He supports this by referring to the services mission statement and quotes the bit about "…preservation of life". There are choral sounds of "mmm" and "that's true" coming from opportunistic career leeches behind him.

His point, if I were asked to summarise, and if I understand it, is that I should have acted in a more 'professional' manner, and that my actions were kamikaze and I could have caused the death of the 'victim' and myself. His argument is convincing. I wonder if I should point out that none of this actually happened, that the victim also happens to be a convicted perpetrator in his own right, and that the incident has been resolved successfully without injury, but I would not be able to match his oratory genius. Defeated, I simply tell him I can see the error of my ways. There is a pause and I anticipate a change of tone, and maybe a grudging congratulations. I wonder perchance if I may *even* get a 'well done' (in the spirit of bravery) but none is forthcoming. As the Governor turns away I consider myself lucky that he is unaware to just what extent the rules have been cuckolded. I decide I would rather live with the stigma of being branded a 'loose cannon', than a 'junkie screw' and keep my mouth clamped until he has departed.

I am patted on the back by my S/O, who I am surprised to see as I hadn't smelt him, and he nods me into his office. On entering I elect to sit in the Talbot recliner and wonder if I am to receive a more personalised, one-to-one kind of bollocking now. I am understandably surprised as the S/O leans over to the evidence safe, punches in his secret 1234 code, and pulls out a bottle of Highland Park Bicentennial Vintage 1977 reserve whiskey.

Paul McMahon – Dead Reckoning

else. There are exceptions to any rule. Think about something else.

To call a shovel a spade:

I almost forget to act suitably gobsmacked upon its production, due to having consumed the odd sneaky sip over the last few weeks. My S/O proclaims he is not a racist man, he hates everybody equally - with the exception of white men. I can see that he hasn't grasped the concept of modern travel or multiculturalism. It is clear to me that he has not realised that the human genome is not interwoven with surnames. I hadn't really thought about it, but I suppose Danny's last name isn't typically British. His criminal tendencies are most definitely linked to his African heritage hence the S/O's current story selection. I sit dutifully and listen - and listen and listen - to stories that would make my hair curl if:

a) I didn't have a uniform shaved head.

b) The laws of physics permitted sound waves to have such an effect on   biological matter.

The first story begins with "This one bastard, black as Newgate's knocker…" the second, "I remember this one darkie, black as the ace of spades…" I really do want to say something about his bigoted attitude. I know I ought to be outraged but he is enjoying himself and I don't want to be rude and interrupt. I don't remember exactly what time I leave.

Red letter day:

I congratulate myself on navigating my way home. I collect my mail from the letter box at the garden door, and shuffle through the envelopes whilst walking to siphon Nick's junk mail off on route, ready to drop them off at his door. His pile is bigger than mine, as usual, which annoys me, like usual. He also has a rather official looking letter in a professional looking thick envelope, like those I see at work. I resist the urge to misplace it in my pile, although mistakes do sometimes happen, and poke them all through his letter box even though the door is ajar enough to simply place them on the mat. That would disturb the natural order of things. I walk up to my front door and enter my flat.

I undress quickly and go through to the front room, to my chair. Once sitting I inspect each envelope and put them in order of importance starting with the least, progressing through to, at the back of the pile, the most important. I count five letters, not including a flyer for a new local Chinese takeaway which I look over first like an entrée.

The next letter is as far as I get. I have never got the order so wrong. It is a cheap envelope, almost see through. It has on it a stamp, as opposed to a frank. Inside is one solitary piece of A4 stencilled paper, the sort that school boys complete their homework on. The paper is folded in half, not concertinaed in thirds as is respectfully done in the business world

I skip to the main body of the letter, excluding the prerequisites of address, opening gambit, and salutation. It consists of one paragraph. On closer inspection, and without any real grammar, it appears to be one long sentence. It reads:

"I hereby give you two weeks' notice to vacate the property you are occupying from the above date as your lease will not be being renewed. I also left an answerphone message seven days ago which you have not seen fit to answer."

I place the letter on my knee and wait for feelings to begin. I am confused, and remain largely unmoved. For want of nothing better to do I raise the letter and read it again. I tut, noticing the senders address on the wrong side of the page. Furthermore, I am fully aware Mrs Porter is an educated lady and I find it hard to believe that she could have missed out some simple punctuation. I conclude therefore that she had not reread the letter before posting it! This in turn implies it was sent in haste, without any real thought or care - a decision as big as this made on a whim! I squint my eyes. How long would it have taken to actually state the date again? How much of her precious ink? I am becoming mildly annoyed. What about the envelope? Anyone could have held it up to a weak sun, and picked out a few key words, negating my *right* to be the first to receive this awful news? And "...be being"? Where was she schooled? I'm successfully out of my chair. The ink is undefined and lazy and I am deliriously happy to discover more ammunition, when closer inspection reveals it is actually a photo copy! This, and my shock at reading the opening line - "To whom it may concern" - really gets me going! I am tearing the letter to pieces and screaming something about me being the only one here.

Paul McMahon – Dead Reckoning

I have had no correspondence with Mrs Porter in the last few years. No obligatory birthday card and no acknowledgment of monies received; nothing since the chair debate. And certainly no fucking answerphone message.

I have postage deducted, 23 days.

I have wine excluded, two quarts of brandy. Let the games commence.

Please fill in this Gap: (Diem perdidi!)

Paul McMahon – Dead Reckoning

A road less travelled:

I bumble hung-over along the road home from work approaching from the opposite direction, (having missed my stop on the bus threefold), with no real purpose in my step, deep within myself. My memory of this morning is limited. I strain my brain trying to wring out a drop of clarity. How did I get to work? I have a vague flashback of early buse, and burning my tongue on a sweet black coffee made for me by Camus A9546AL. I recall Gav locking me in the office on the Landing for a mandatory kip and then not a lot until feeding the beasts at Lunchtime. Very clear however is the pool cue I received to the face toward the end of the day. The reason is not so clear, but I presume it would have had something to do with my attitude to the cons. I have another gap on the internal hard drive, this time courtesy of the red mist. Unfortunate really as I am reliably informed I was a credit to my uniform, assisted no doubt by the pain-numbing qualities of Chateauneuf-du-Pape and my new personal issue - Landlady-rage - I'm carrying with me. I pause next to a verge of grass as I have run out of motivation. I may just as well stop here as anywhere else.

My lip doesn't hurt as much as I thought it would. It only stretches the elastic scab when the corners of my mouth move away and up toward my ears, which lately isn't happening with any degree of frequency, thankfully. In the absence of any inspiration I set off again from whence I came this morning, and detour past the bail hostel on the way to observe the oiks going about their oikdom in the grounds of this beautiful old Georgian building. A particularly inebriated German (giveaway handlebar moustache) is travelling in my direction, moving quickly and angular, in the way that people do in the latter stages of falling over to avoid the inevitable impact with a few extra quick paces. He collapses directly in my path and I hear a noise that sounds like it should be the phonetic spelling for 'severe injury' and I continue walking. Who am I to intercede in this man's mission? He is where he wants to be presumably. Besides I have enough to deal with myself at this

Paul McMahon – Dead Reckoning

moment in time; in my left hand I grip my copy of the local rag, so I can trawl the property pages upon my return to my depressingly temporary abode. As I step over the German I hear him shout something which I don't catch. It is not until I am a good deal further down the road that I realise that was my old landing cleaner, Kafka, shouting my name. I would go back and help him, but according to PSO 1215 and the code of conduct I am not supposed to associate with ex-prisoners. It's regrettable. Think about something else.

I stop at the newsagents to peer into the window at the flat adverts. I systematically navigate my way round twelve adverts for local masseuses and escorts in search of the miniscule accommodation section. The man standing next to me is reading cards also; I hope he doesn't think that I'm looking for a hooker. I feel great relief when at last I find a solitary card advertising a flat share! I would never consider this, but I go to great lengths to place my finger on the tiny card and make a show of taking the phone number down with a pen that I huff and puff over retrieving from my pocket. He is not looking so I resort to reading out some choice words as I write them down, "En suite, inc bills". That should do it. To my amazement the man next to me asks if he may borrow my pen. I offer it to him and marvel at him taking down a number for a local call girl named 'Mandy'. He hands the pen back, thanks me and walks off. I stand for a bit and watch him advance off into the distance, not moving out of the way for anyone. I think how different we are. That in this moment I wish I *am* him; answerable to no-one, my behaviour unkempt, no scale of values measured against a higher power. My lip is hurting.

Got up left foot forward:

I have mixed feelings about waking up this morning. It isn't that I ever resent my body for becoming bored of its perpendicular-ness but that I would like to be consulted first, be given the opportunity to object. What if one day, I conclude rationally, that I wish to cease this practise? What then? After all, I am supposed to be in charge of me. I grumpily realise that this cerebral dialogue must mean that I am suffering with a greater degree of awakedom than I first thought, bringing about my first audible contribution to the day:

Me: Uuuuuuuuuuuuuuurrrrggggggggggg

I run a diagnostic on my mood and discover that it is very, very bad news indeed. I crash into bathroom to debate it out. I don't immediately recognise my reflection. My face is puffy and erupting in grog-blossoms all over its surface. My skin is a little yellow but I am sure this will come off after I have submerged myself in the bath. My mouth is sticky so I choose to remedy this by brushing my teeth. Combining the brush and paste is complicated, however, by the fact both my hands are trembling. My accommodation anxiety must be causing all of this. I don't need the toilet and can't remember what I have come in here for.

I eyeball myself in the mirror.

Paul McMahon – Dead Reckoning

Time to Face Facts:

Face.
Face facts.
Clear as the nose on it.
Mood's written all over it.
Bulldog. Wasp.
Scream
till I'm
blue in
it.

She's laughing in it.
Can't keep a straight one.
Nose off despite it.

It's not just a pretty one.
Don't get egg on it.
Save it.
Put a brave one on it.

I am distracted from my ranting by the exhausting of that musty little reservoir of air at the bottom of the lungs that never gets used, except in moments of frenzy or delirium. How great it feels to expel it, let it fulfil its destiny. I gasp in sharply to replenish and this intake is so clean. Purifyingly so. That must have been the rage escaping. That must be where it sits, dwelling in the stale bottom there.

Paul McMahon – Dead Reckoning

I'm pink therefore I'm spam:

I decide that the tattooed proprietor of this hardware shop would not be enthusiastic about my existentialist realisation that my entire life's choices had brought me here, to this row of this backstreet premises looking at this 185mm heavy duty straight bar hasp. Or how, only last week, I was talking to an experienced looter of premises about the very subject of door barricades. So I decide not to share my philosophising with him. Instead I opt for asking him hundreds of questions, and commandeering him as my personal shopping assistant - a service I don't think this store has previously provided.

Considering I have been the only person in here for the last hour I don't think he is focused enough on my prospective custom, especially as I am looking to purchase rather a lot of equipment. This leads me to suspect another revenue stream. I wonder if he obtains the majority of his business through the products on show, or if he has a rife under-the-counter trade in kiddie porn. It would explain the pony tail. No matter, I am preoccupied.

Know one's onions:

After a while his novel approach to customer service is to throw me a pile of trade product literature he has out back in order for me to peruse at my leisure, and he retreats behind the counter. I occasionally have to come back to the counter from the small wooden stool he has furnished me with at the opposite end of the shop, in order to ask for translations on the more technical phrasings, like which components are 'armour shielded'? And which is superior, the 'special', or 'mushroom' pin? This he explains without looking up, seemingly engrossed in something at floor level

Paul McMahon – Dead Reckoning

behind the counter and grinding his teeth. I am tempted to ask him if he has anything more risqué to offer me. I take stock and see I am amassing quite a set of accessories; the lock I am looking at currently has 22 million possible combinations with six space positions and six depth positions. I wonder if this will be complex enough to outdo a privately educated landlady.

The pony-tailed one calls "last orders" as I am quibbling over the benefits of the 'salt-spray corrosion test' on this UL437-Listed high security lock and whether it would offer much benefit in my case. Feeling the pressure of time I decide I should opt for this added feature, just in case, and approach the paedophile with an arm full of apparatus. He seems genuinely pleased as I dump my goods onto the counter, either in anticipation of getting rid of me or possibly because the sale of these items will enable him to fund his seedy pursuits, whatever they are. I am sure I catch him smile a noncey smile.

It occurs to me en route home that I should formulate some sort of plan - or at least put a little thought into possible outcomes - and not blindly stagger into this operation without investing any time in the 'pre' stage for fear of regretting it in the 'post' stage. With this in mind I decide I should stop off for a rest next to the off licence. It's approximately half way, give or take a small detour, and I haven't seen what's-her-name for a while so I really should say hello. I exit laden even more so with a bottle of Jim Beam (White) and a small bottle of Barley-Wine.

To be in Dulcarnon:

On the table I've cleared I'm moving characters around to help me visualise the proceedings. I have constructed the set out of random possessions. The doorway to the flat is built from three books: the side supports are hardcover copies of *One Flew Over the Cuckoo's Nest* and *On the Road*, for they're both the same height, and the top of the frame I've made from a relatively thick paper back AA venue booklet. I am represented by my glass, currently half-empty with brandy, this side of the door and Mrs Porter portrayed by the bottle of half-full Brandy on the other. I recline in my chair and await inspiration.

The inescapable fact of the matter is that I *cannot* afford to rent elsewhere; I can't really afford the rent here, or to repair the mysterious array of fist-sized holes in the plaster board which periodically materialise around the flat after a night on the whiskey. Not to mention stumping up another £500 deposit on a *new* place as there is no way that Mrs Porter is going to return my deposit when she sees the state of the flat. I can't go through a letting agency as my credit is so appallingly bad, and I have no idea where my Passport or personal documents are. I just know they are not here. A private flat share is not going to work; I can't share a cell. If I were a con I am sure the reception staff would make me 'high-risk cell share' on the risk assessment due to the fact that I get frustrated easily and have a history of alcohol abuse. Also any landlord is going to want a reference and I don't think Mrs Porter would play ball. No, I *know* Mrs Porter won't play ball.

Arc of visibility:

After a depressing 40 minute appraisal of my current situation I notice that all that has happened 'plan wise' is that the majority of the brandy has moved from one receptacle to the other. I consider this a good omen as the balance of power has shifted and therefore think it a worthwhile exercise. In the absence of anything else positive to take from it I declare it a resounding success and pour another brandy, draining Mrs Porter dry. I can't plan for variables I do not know. I can only deal with what's this side of the horizon. Think about something else.

Taking minutes:

I am taking an interest in detail, as people do when they are trying to prevent *other* people talking to them, by giving off an air of being too preoccupied to interact with. I am doing this by squiggling random squiggles on my note pad and poking my tongue out of the corner of my mouth in mock concentration. I need only conduct myself in this manner until I get out of the staff morning meeting and up to my landing. The reason being I am not entirely sure if I am capable of speech. As the floor is offered round to us foot soldiers. I shake my head, and am the first up and out of the door in a wholly out of context burst of kinetic-ness.

Groundswell:

Hangovers always liberate the profound part of my brain. Looking out over Gavs and my landing I feel like a weak salmon swimming up tide. Gav is oblivious to it all and I seem to be the only person who can see what's actually happening here. We have no sooner than we have finished unlocking I'm watching bags of protein powder and tins of tuna being moved around our landing from cell to cell like this is a fucking Sunday market. In every cell search I do on this landing I find mobile phone top up numbers written on scraps of paper that have undoubtedly been used to buy smack, and loose foil wrappers with streaks of heroin on them between book pages. There is hardly anybody awake. Most of the landing are sleeping all day, some hovering on the brink of a coma with any luck, and those that are awake are at the medication hatch arguing with the nurse for whatever tablet that they can 'cheek' or regurgitate and sell later for more smack. The remaining few are looking dodgy, scuttling disorientated from cell to cell, constantly itching and twitching with runny noses, dry mouths and needle-point pupils, covering every square inch of the landing looking for fag-butts - everywhere except the showers, dirty apathetic fuckers. We seem to be breeding these junkies. Some shit-bag con must have come into reception from court with a major parcel of gear up his arse. It's the only explanation. I'll find the fucker and wipe him out. I wouldn't mind so much but this is making me look bad and is damaging my sense of pride. I don't like these fuckers getting one past me, even if I seem to be the only one who can see it. Gav tells me I'm paranoid. Some of these bastards have come in for the first time, clean, on a 14 day non-payment of fines sentence, and are going to walk out the gate after seven with a brand new habit that needs feeding and a network of thieving contacts only too happy to get them in on the action. The revolving door is born; good old rehabilitation. No wonder the prison population is going through the fucking roof.

Born with a silver spoon in his hand

I am confronted by the lone figure of a spindly, dirty, hollow-checked, yellow-fingered, old-aged youngster of about god knows how old. He is wearing a vest and ripped dark-coloured jeans so crusty that they look like they're supporting his weight of their own volition. He has greasy, matted, dark locks and there are intravenous track marks all over his bare arms from collapsed veins. An A-grade Junkie. A Lesser Spotted Crackhead of the first degree. I call Gav over without delay to marvel at our new exhibit. Step right up for the main attraction. I point out his clothes and Gav asks if he is "…a Binner? Hobo? Vagrant?" What happens now I will only be able to do justice to in the fullness of time.

Paul McMahon – Dead Reckoning

The circus freak opens his mouth, takes in a breath, and lets out a perfectly pronounced, exquisite example of the Queen's English. What a juxtaposition of sight and sound. How incongruous. What a fucking diamond. I have no idea exactly what he says as I am too absorbed in the melody.

After a long pause he breaks the silence to ask about his toilet roll; I toss him his arse paper and ask him his name. He replies in a romantic melancholy way that his name is "David Temple-Jones".

I am struggling with myself on the way back to the office as I can't help but be amused by the newbie and *almost* like him. This new feeling quickly dissipates when I receive a call from the desk that "Temple-Jones" is on self-harm watch. Now I hate him. I wish he would fuck off and die and save me this mass of paperwork. Inconsiderate cunt.

Dead Ringer:

The morning passes without incident and I elect to eat my lunch on the landing to avoid the S/O's. The only drawback to being secluded up here is that I have to look in on the self-harmers in the middle of the lunch hour. This is a small price to pay for getting through the day undercover. I eat half my sandwich, half my crisps and drink half my drink. This being half way through lunch time I get up and wander round the six on books that I have. Back and almost into my sandwich, I remember that I have Temple-Jones and so go back to A3-31 to check. Temple-Jones Is lying on the top bunk recognisable only by his filthy dreads sprouting out of the bed end nearest the door. There is also some random straining

Paul McMahon – Dead Reckoning

going on behind the loose toilet sheet. Evidently a mammoth expenditure from his cell mate; I must leave time for one myself.

I am woken up at exactly 14:00hrs by Gav, via the method of a paper cut to the corners of the mouth as he slides the unlock list into said orifice. Gav apologises profusely, an apology somewhat nullified by the gigantic smirk and splutters of intermittent giggling. Taking it on the chin, I bristle off to begin the unlocking when I am alerted to a cell on my right by loud banging, the sound of which would be in keeping with a sizable panic.

Place your bets:

On route I try and predict the goings on behind the door. I decide to bet all-in that it's a vicious assault and 'call it' on the way, Gav has evidently reached the same conclusion (though not quick enough) as he is at the door first, smiling with his stave drawn. Entry is made hard by the cause of the banging. Blocking the doorway is a filthy Yardie, almost obscured by his sticky dreadlocks, screaming and pointing at the sheet covering the toilet. Pulling back the sheet exposes D.T. Jones. His neck is connected by a novel use of a bed sheet to the window frame. A hairy doppelganger.

I recognise the bowline knot immediately as I tie it with exactly the same faux pas - not dressing it correctly. A standard slip knot would have been more fit for purpose, as it has a built-in failsafe provided by its constricting nature, in case the drop itself were not sufficient to do the job in an instant. The bowline and it's cousin the butterfly knot, although strong knots, are static loops and leave open the possibility of a 30 minute dangling - and nobody likes to see that.

Paul McMahon – Dead Reckoning

After this, therefore because of it:

The filthy Yardie is still screaming behind me, fraggling out and knocking into me making it impossible for me to concentrate. For the good of D.T. Jones (and as a lesson not to have identical dreadlocks and almost cost me my job) I elect to punch him squarely in the face. This resolves the issue and leaves me free to get on with the job in hand - being saving my job...(and D.T. Jones).

I wrap my arms round his thighs so his navel is level with my eyes and raise him up to take the pressure off his throat. Gav unfastens his fish knife and begins to saw away at the ligature connecting his neck to the window.

It is at this point the moisture begins to seep through the material of his jeans and onto the breast of my shirt. It is also becoming apparent that the other side of Temple-Jones is also damp and oozing against my forearms. Gav severs the last of the rig and the carcass flops onto me. At this point I am more concerned about my shirt than any head injury so I drop him on the floor, thus negating any more seepage.

The next moments are like a Mexican standoff with each of us waiting for the other to draw their face mask to perform CPR on D.T. Jones. Gav 'John Wayne's' me, whispers "your turn" and whips out his radio to notify the Emergency Control Room and request assistance, etc., etc. Clever, as this leaves me just standing there jobless; being jobless doesn't go down well in a coroner's court. Admitting defeat I draw my mask and kneel over D.T. Jones, threatening him that if he doesn't wake up. I'm going to "fucking kill" him.

Once D.T Jones is loaded into the ambulance, Gav and I return to the wing. Where we are greeted with admiring silence. Someone asks if Gav is ok. He replies that he is "a bit upset that the look-alike bastard raised the alarm" as he had a bet that "...the posh boy wouldn't last the week". This statement is ignored by the S/O as Gav is "in shock", and can't really mean it as he has "...just saved his life". I wonder if the same leniency will apply to me if the posh lad snuffs it. I can't recall which bed and which hairstyle was which.

David Jones' Locker:

I am given the task of securing the cell with a member of the security department, in case D.T. Jones dies and an investigation is needed; I genuinely hope doesn't happen as I hate investigations. I open the door to relocate the cell mate, whilst explaining my earlier actions were for the greater good. I allow him time to identify and collect his own possessions, which he does rapidly. I ask him if there is anything in the locker that belongs to him. He replies that the contents belonged to the "swinger". I take a look inside and see one solitary envelope with a stamp and address on the front. The post isn't collected until later on today so I slip it unseen into my pocket and tell the security officer to seal up the cell as it is. The cell may be left like this some time, and the envelope may contain a birthday card. I suppose it is the least I can do really.

This task completed I am sent home despite my assertions that I am fit for duty and don't want to let the team down. On the way off the wing I am annoyed that this will make me look weak, and snap at the care and welfare nurse when she asks me if I am

Paul McMahon – Dead Reckoning

okay. I wonder if I am being sent home for reasons of negligence but no one has said anything to me. I walk with purpose and a slight glare all the way out of work, and all the way to the 'Lord Nelson'.

Nothing is certain but death and taxes:

I am at the searching-pockets-for-loose-change stage, being that every time I've brought a round I have thrown the change in a different pocket with abandon. I order myself another scotch and a pint and start the increasingly difficult task of counting out the right money. As I throw the remaining change into my right pocket I feel something in there, other than the house keys that have made that pocket their own over the years. I slowly wobble back to my table and put the remainder of my pint which has survived the journey down. The scotch didn't make it off the bar as I thought I might spill it. Think about something else.

I knock down the receiver to the pay phone next to me and dial the front desk of A-wing. Gollum answers the phone. He must have been 'jobbed-in' to cover either me or Gav in our absence. He is probably in place of Gav. Think about something else. I ask him if there is any news on the swinger. Gollum replies excitedly that, "Yeah, he's died." I thank Gollum for his respectful telephone manner and he realises like a twat who it is he is speaking to. Whilst he is proclaiming his sorrow I ask him if he has met my mate 'Tone' and hang up.

Paul McMahon – Dead Reckoning

Exhibit A:

I pull out the letter, and inspect the addressees; "Mum and dad". The address is in Kensington. Nice part of town. Without any sense of ceremony, I slip out the paper contained within and unfold it.

The main body of the text reads;

to me *"Mum, Dad, in this letter I am going to tell you how much you mean*

David"

Is it finished? There is a gap, an empty void. What does it mean? Is that the point? Did he feel empty toward them? I'll never

Paul McMahon – Dead Reckoning

know. I don't understand. They might not understand. They will have to live with that for the rest of their lives. I can't have that.

His final words in hand. I am a voice box.

I am no good with words. Besides there is no way I could replicate the swirly italic handwriting that D.T Jones has flowered up the first two lines of the page with. I decide to become an editor for the greater good.

So after some thought I draw a knot.

"Mum, Dad, in this letter I am going to tell you how much you mean to me

David"

It is the 'True Loves' knot. I don't think it needs the title though. The knot looks like what they will want to feel. How they will have wished he felt. It will occupy a little of the void that the D.T Jones left. I wish I could feel this knot.

Paul McMahon – Dead Reckoning

<u>St Boniface's cup:</u>

I revisit the bar and mumble a silent toast "here's to absent cons". I don't know why I do this; to me he is just a number. I do feel something peculiar for the parents though, a sort of sorrow, a sort of guilt. I hope I have helped their grief a little and they should know that somebody raised a glass for him. They don't deserve this. Nobody deserves a cowardly dead son. Nobody.

"…Here's to the posh junkie" I say out loud, and I leave in search of a post box.

<u>Homecoming:</u>

I arrive at the ground floor entrance and make hard work of gaining access. Once in, I shut the door and stumble over to Nick's front door which is open as usual. He is sat in his chair and looks like shit, like he has been there for days, fucking waster. He hasn't changed out of his crusty dressing gown either, and he is on the drink again, Unemployment has hit him hard evidently. Seeing as though he hasn't noticed me I sneakily bend over him to ease the glass out of his hand. I haven't had a drink all bus journey and he looks smashed.

<u>Like an Owl in an Ivy bush:</u>

Nicks sapient, vacant look is pretty normal when he's drunk so this doesn't concern me. It isn't even when Nick doesn't let go of his glass or now I feel how cold is hand that I worry - these thinks can be explained away after a few drinks - but I smell a rat when I notice one of the little fuckers moving around under

Nicks dressing gown and him not so much as flinching. It's now I realise we might have a problem.

I sit down next to Nick on the sofa in silence. I do not feel scared. I do feel deep sadness. I do feel empty. I sit like this until the light outside has all but vanished and I can see no further than the open door step. I know this will be last time we will get to spend in each other's company and I want it to last for ever. I notice from this angle that there is no lock on the inside of the door. I had up until now thought the permanently open door was a welcoming gesture. It upsets me that I may have entered like I did when Nick wanted to be alone. That he might not have felt confident enough to ask me to leave. I pick up the phone to call the police but there is no ring tone. There is no food to speak of in any of the cupboards. There is no washing powder under the sink, no photos on any of the walls. An unsettling thought seeps into my consciousness that I didn't really know Nick at all.

I try to think of a time when we discussed day-to-day life - where we brought our groceries, What he did for a living - as opposed to the relevance of religion in war torn countries, which is the most important of our senses, or who was the hardest of Chaos' sons, Erebus or Night?

To appease his Manes:

I am angry that no-one has noticed his passing, that people have walked past the door to our building all weekend and no one has bothered to engage him, that I haven't bothered to engage him. Even when I was here for him I wasn't actually here for *him*.

Paul McMahon – Dead Reckoning

I still can't bring myself to disturb him. He looks so peaceful sitting there. I pour me and Nick another drink and nestle the glass back into his hand. I tell Nick about my dilemma, and about my dream of the coast. There is nobody else I can talk to and I would have loved to have opened up to Nick about my problems. Nick has been a good listener. I rise and tell Nick to enjoy his drink, bow my head and let the man get on with it, jamming the door firmly shut with the rug on the way out.

St Martin:

There is a break while the tape is changed. So I take a chance to analyse the proceedings. If I was to say the word eponymous over and over and over and over again, eventually it would cease to make any sense. It would evolve into a mere sound, just a bizarre meaningless rhythmic bluuur, In much the same way that me endlessly repeating my reasons for not reporting Nick's death have begun to make them sound utterly nonsensical. Even to my Brief. This I quietly acknowledge to myself is a slightly worrying development.

Evidently someone had missed Nick. His passing had made a difference. His non-contribution to the world had been noticed by someone. It is explained to me that one of the bin men had noticed a pungent smell (which I can give testament to) coming from around Nick's flat. This isn't odd in its self. What is 'odd', according to the bin man's statement, is that he was surprised at being able to open the garden door without having to struggle against and compress bags of rubbish behind it. Furthermore, the area directly outside Nick's door was "uncommonly clean"; the door which he had never seen in any position other than wide open, was jammed shut with a rug; and there was, to his expert nose, no explanation for the pong.

I accept this and ask the detective if she might pass on my thanks to the bin man. She appears not to have understood what I am saying. I am speaking the language of Martin.

My brief, Mr Martin, is surprisingly talented for a publicly supplied lawyer. I do not want to trouble the Union, and I would prefer it not to be all round the staff-mess in the morning. The rumour mill is fully manned and in perfect working order.

I consult Mr Martin briefly, to get a third eye on how things are going. He says in a voice only I can hear that things are going ok, and that I should just stick to the truth. This is good advice, as the truth is I am guilty of nothing but breaking the law. Therefore I state, "I apologise for not reporting Nick's death, but I didn't want anyone to disturb him."

Apparently this is good enough for the detective. After the tape is stopped she goes on to explain that there is no question of foul play, that Nick had died from a massive over dose of sodium fluoride, this being the active ingredient in rat poison. His fingerprints are all over the canister, and all over a bottle of vodka found next to it. Also, a "Nick" who had been on first name terms with staff at the Samaritans helpline had that morning said he was going to top himself. Pretty conclusive stuff. She explains that this interview was in accordance with procedure, and that she was hopeful that that could be the end of the matter.

I can't help be slightly annoyed at the fact Nick had a bottle of vodka stashed away without my knowledge, and even more put out when the detective reports to me, in answer to my question, that it was Grey Goose Vodka. Selfish little bastard.

I am surprised when I am ushered back into a holding cell post interview. The kind Desk Sergeant furnishes me with a black coffee, and explains it is just untill morning.

You are what you eat:

I am stood in the hallway looking out to sea. The coastal shots don't seem so calming with the thud of hammer and grind of saw. The builders are out downstairs and there is a rare window of quiet. I resent the fact that the work started before Nick was in the ground, that it probably started before he was fully digested even. It doesn't seem right. This lot seem to be at it 24 hours a day. I would complain but it wouldn't do any good. She has all but evicted me.

It is early and I should be making the most of the chance to sleep, but I can't stop thinking about the rats. There is at least one little bastard scuttling around with Nick's DNA inside it. It has probably developed bad eyesight and an aversion to washing. I wonder if I would recognise it. Or maybe it's dead. Maybe it has died from all the rat poison - maybe they will all die - and Nick will have defeated the bastards Post-Mortem. Maybe that was the self-sacrificial plan. It is a nice thought. Think about something else.

Mourning person:

I regain some sort of concentration in the hallway. I walk out from here - into here. Looking around the kitchen I sigh at the dirty plates on the worktop and lazily scratch my naked arse. Whatever time it is I'm sure that it's too early to be clothed and besides, I am so dreadfully attended this morning that there hardly seems any point getting dressed. I have no intention of interacting with anyone, so I needn't worry about etiquette. I slowly tear off a bin liner and slide the soiled plates into the sack. The food was dried right onto them, and the pepper sauce had probably stained the bowl. They would have to have been thrown away out anyway. Think about something else. With that job half-done, I stop, having run out of enthusiasm, and return from whence I had come to lay down. There wasn't any point getting up. There doesn't seem much point lying down either, but one must do something.

The nuts and bolts of it:

My plan hasn't progressed itself in my absence. I was hoping that it would have organically materialised in the back of my head without me having to invest any more thought in it. I thought my work was done at its initial conception, but that sadly appears not to be the case. It is still at the stage I left it at my last decision, spluttering to a halt at the 'just refuse to move-out and then' stage. To my credit though, I have acted on what little I have decided. Having refused to relocate, I have barricaded up the door so well even Oily would bounce straight off it.

I am inspecting my handiwork now. The door is finished. Not being able to choose between them, and not wanting to miss out on any of the benefits, I have elected to fit four new locks. Equally spaced are 1 x Yale 89, 1 x Chubb 3G114E, 1 x Union 21068 (KXT) APG Lock, and 1 x Cisa electric rim lock, all individually covered by an Asec Anti-Thrust Plate. To check the identity of any prospective visitor I have taken the liberty of installing a covert 200 degree door viewer, and have accessorised with a Chubb WS6 Door Chain between locks one and two, and an Ingersol DSC2 Door Check between locks three and four. The look is completed by a Dual-Function Security Bar supporting the middle of the door wedged, as per instructions, against the floor 28 inches away. I will say with a certain degree of confidence that this door should be capable of resisting the entry attempts of an elderly eight stone landlady. In its souped-up state it is probably harder to breech than the walls surrounding it. Good work.

The only other point of access is the small window I hang my stinking boots out of overlooking the fire escape up to the front door. I am loathed to ever close this as it keeps the flat airy. Pondering this, it occurs to me that first of all I need to keep the flat kept, so a swinglock locking window hasp with alarm it is then. Granted she would have to scale the side of the building in order to stand a chance at squeezing through it, but where there's a will there's a way.

There is nothing good or bad but thinking makes it so:

I decide to give myself a deadline in an attempt to motivate my grey matter. I propose to myself that I should have at least one option put down on paper before the day is out. I clear everything with a distracting quality out of the lounge. These things range from the radio to a pot plant. I am finding it so increasingly difficult to concentrate that I can hear the bloody thing growing. My cerebral cortex needs as much help as it can get to do its thing. Come on son, don't let me down now.

Some way into my task, something dawns upon me. Thinking is a dangerous pursuit. I mean really thinking….and I mean really dangerous. It can be irrecoverably damaging. If I were going about my daily business, actively involved in actually doing something, I wouldn't be thinking about the best way to dispose of a body or have drawn a doodle of a dead landlady.

Paul McMahon – Dead Reckoning

To number the sands:

It seems an impossible task; to actually make a decision completely on my own about what to do. I'm not entirely sure what I am supposed to be thinking about? I have spent the last 45 minutes accomplishing nothing. The product of all this mental wrangling is another doodle, this time of a complex key. In a change of tactics I decide to rattle off the first thing that comes into my head. If it works for Michael Stipe then it will surely work for me. What comes out is not a rival to the stream of consciousness that is "The End of the World As We Know It", but it is in its own right perfect. My military strategy for the Old Lady is to simply do nothing. I will assume a 'detached Buddha tactic' to confuse and befuddle her. Genius like this deserves a drink. So I go out.

Liquid Logic:

I am at the stage where I know I have had enough to drink. I am still able to order in a clear, concise manner what I want from the bar of this random pub I don't know the name of, and stop myself repeating myself, but I still realise that I *am* drunk. Normal folk drunk. Even at this juncture I appreciate that I probably won't be able to remember all the intricacies of what has happened so far tonight, but the big things I will recollect no problem. I am sat here at the bar, opposite a coffee machine, and know the sensible thing to do would be to order a double espresso and take a sobering fresh-air walk home whilst I am still compos mentis enough to comprehend that I don't live on a ship in Balham. I spend a little time reflecting on how ill I always feel in the morning, and how I have yet still to try and navigate the incredibly complicated front door locks I fitted earlier today - without s sober dry run. The fact

Paul McMahon – Dead Reckoning

that I have apportioned time to deliberate all of this in a rational, relatively sober-ish sort of a way makes my graduation onto the top shelf even more indefensible. I do this a lot. In my own uniquely manipulative way, as the barman pours me a Double Captain Morgan I tell myself that, seeing as I am being such an irresponsible prick, I might as well teach myself a damn good lesson and get completely wasted so I feel absolutely bloody awful in the morning. Alcohol gives my logic certain liquidity.

Bacchus a noye plus d'hommes que Neptune (The Ale house wrecks more souls than the ocean):

I don't do too much soul-searching after the top shelf as I'm caught up thinking I'm having a good time. A little introspection creeps in again, however, when I have a little unexpected down time and have cause to stand under the Hand dryer with my open jean crotch pushed up to the hot air blower, having had an accident. The accident was caused by not being able to comprehend that the button fly on my jeans was not a zip and, after cracking the puzzle, not having the dexterity to unleash the beast in time. Right now the door opens and a fellow patron walks in the lavatory. Sensing that an explanation is immediately appropriate the only thing I can think to say turns out to be,

Me: I'm not fucking it, honestly.

When people tell you they're being honest, it is a generally accepted truism that they are in fact being dishonest. Seeing as though the poor fellow only has a fraction of a second to take in the scene before the body's natural reaction to revulsion forces him to look away, he really *can't* be blamed for reading the situation wrongly. What he *can* be blamed for is the volley of insults he fires at me afterwards whilst he is having a piss. What I *can't* be blamed for is taking this unwarranted abuse badly. What I *can* be blamed for is pushing him in to the urinal so hard he bursts his nose on the tiles above. What the landlord *can't* be blamed for is taking exception to the added work this bloody mess has caused him. However, what the landlord simply *must* be blamed for is speaking to me so disrespectfully that he forces me to leave without paying my tab as I'm so offended. Think about something else.

Your guess is as good as mine:

Here we are again.

I think it's a weekend as the hustle and bustle outside my front room window on the high street is rather more frantic than usual. I don't know what the last thing I remember is, so I decide to begin the ritual of going through my phone and checking my pockets. Helpfully enough I appear to have conked out in the vicinity of my jeans, which are hanging above me over the door. I'm irritated as they appear to have a gaping tear in them and are filthy. Oooops. I force my arm off the floor, just enough to reach a strand of cotton emanating from the trouser leg, and tug until they relinquish their grip on the door and fall directly onto my head. Normally I would find this kind of thing amusing, but I am distracted in mid fall by the sight of my legs and the resultant realisation that I am actually wearing my only pair of jeans. I don't know why I didn't feel their wetness earlier.

Paul McMahon – Dead Reckoning

I hold my breath and listen out for any sound, any tell-tale signs that someone else is here. Breathing, snoring, pottering about...anything. With nothing audible forthcoming, I sniff the air for anything alien to me, a faint smell of perfume or aftershave perhaps? Nothing...nothing that can overpower this waft of urine I'm caked in anyway.

Happy enough, I arch my back and peel off my soaking wet jeans and boxer shorts. Naked I stand up, the blood rushing to my head and unleashing a pounding rhythm as I head for the bathroom, paying mind not to step on the young lady in the door way...

Jimmy riddle:

Who is she? What the hell does she think she's doing partially obscuring my lino? Why is she naked? Is she dead? She is lying on her back and I'm stuck standing with one foot either side of her, this being the point in my stagger to the loo that I've discovered her. And so I stand frozen, neither in the bathroom nor out. It is at this moment I realise how desperate I am to evacuate my bladder and I have to take hold of my privates in a sort of consoling way, communicating to him that there are far more pressing matters at hand by gripping the end and pressing my hand.

It is here and now, with me standing straddling her, cock in hand, that she decides to wake up.

To her credit she hasn't been unoriginal and screamed. We are staring straight at each other equally stunned. There is a moment of stillness and I am unsure what the best course of action is to take. She doesn't move a muscle either.

Paul McMahon – Dead Reckoning

For want of anything better to say I go for a jovial "good morning". It is obvious that she isn't going to be cajoled by good manners when she kicks my testicles back inside my body. Her ball-splitting kick is followed by my ear-splitting scream. Unoriginal maybe, but very necessary.

I now have my own close up of the lino and have assumed the foetal position. I feel physically onomatopoeic like this, as I have always led a cloistered existence. She on the other hand is very much upright and at the front door, screaming at it for its unwillingness to open.

As the pain subsides, I'm able to recognise that the sight of a naked woman trying to run out into the street as being somewhat comical and, forgetting myself for a second let, out an incongruous little giggle. This hasn't gone down well. I suppose it isn't the volume of the giggle that she's noticed in amongst all her cursing and screeching, but the type of sound it was - totally out of context, like a brief whiff of faeces in a cake factory. Her frenzy has moved up a gear. I can tell this by the look on her face and by the fact that she is coming toward me brandishing a running shoe in her left hand. If one has any say in what type of implement you are beaten with I recommend a shoe, and if one has one's pick of shoes, I highly recommend a running shoe. The shock absorbing qualities are unparalleled as far as being the victim is concerned. I anticipate I could stand quite a lashing with this.

She stops, more out of a lack of cardio than an abatement of hatred for me as far as I can tell. Either that or she realised her weapon selection is poor. She backs off a little and leans up against the door to regain her breath.

Exhausted, she brushes her hair out of her face to reveal a gaunt jaw line and a pasty complexion. She has track marks along her right arm and one or two lesions on her legs, which could do with a shave in my view. I hadn't noticed her slim physique and

Paul McMahon – Dead Reckoning

pert breasts whilst she was leathering me. Buying into stereotypes I begin to wonder:

1)   Have I had sex with a hooker?
2)   If so, have I paid her already, as they are a rather unscrupulous bunch?

I ask her who she is and how she got into my flat. I don't see what's funny about this, so I'm confused when she laughs, growing in volume into a bonafide cackle. I let the laughing run its course, as I don't really have anything to add.

Ka Me Ka Thee:

She explains to me that she had popped into the down stairs yard last night, to smoke some crack "in peace", when I had ruined her tranquillity by stumbling through my own back gate and falling flat on my face at the bottom of the fire escape. Having certain a business acumen, she had thereafter brokered some sort of intoxicated deal whereby she would escort me up to the flat in return for payment. Once inside, what she hadn't foreseen was the complexity of the door mechanisms and the volume of liquor I had consumed. These two factors meant that she could not vacate the flat herself, or get enough sense out of me to assist her in doing so either. Realising that she was going to be incarcerated overnight she explains how she settled down to a few rocks, a bit of TV and a nice hot bath. The resulting combination of steam and crack cocaine apparently explains her collapsed position this morning on the border between the hall and the bathroom.

Paul McMahon – Dead Reckoning

It would appear that she has totally forgotten she is naked, either that or she is completely comfortable with this arrangement as she isn't holding her belly in or covering her nipples - like me. Manners dictate that it would be very bad form to get an erection in these circumstances, but I can't help looking at her nether regions as she is seated, knees drawn up just like me, her lady garden eyeballing me.

Hoist the flag:

I begin to get that little twitching sensation, like a group of dockworkers are hoisting up my sail little by little, and realise that I either need to think about my grandmother or engage her in a distracting line of conversation in order to fix her gaze with mine. I ask her if she received payment for her troubles last night, to which she rather obviously states that she hasn't. I declare that I will recompense her for her troubles and apologise for holding her captive. She magnanimously thanks me for the loan of the bath tub and the use of the flat, and stands offering me her hand to help me up. It is all very civil.

I calculate that I'm probably about half-mast and that I may be able to get away with it unnoticed after all, so I accept the outstretched hand and rise. As I stand she drops down to her knees and takes my penis in her mouth. It would seem she mistook my assertion that I would reimburse her for her troubles as some sort of subtle street request for fellatio. It would be rude to correct her at this stage; she may get embarrassed, so to spare her feelings I let her continue. Think about something else.

Paul McMahon – Dead Reckoning

I can think about nothing else as this activity nears its end other than that I want this young lady to stay here for the rest of my life, cold sores and all. It is not until the pursuit is over that I begin to wish desperately that I knew where the keys were and that I had agreed a price prior to embarking on the last few minutes. What a turn around. While she is in the bathroom I take the opportunity to go up into the lounge and take a few pound notes out of her jeans to pay her with. I also take the flat keys out of the same pocket. She must have been confused. No doubt the cash is mine and I am not being taken for a mug in my own home. Besides, I think that is very reasonable rate for a B&B. She seems happy with £20, so I pocket the other £20 I was holding back for the bartering. Once I have conquered the front door for her she goes on her merry way, pleasantly threatening to bump into me again.

86'ed:

The bus driver overshoots the bus stop by at least 15 feet this evening. I retaliate by giving him incorrect change, forcing him to delve into his pocket and shuffle through some coins to retrieve a near worthless one for me. Retribution complete; I am able to take my ticket in a moderately good mood still thanks to my quick thinking. This sense of tranquillity lasts all the way to my front door. Even the local hood rats silently shooting each other in the road with their finger fire-arms can't ruin it for me. A quick time check reveals it is 21:46hrs. Hopefully one of them will get run over tonight as the fog is thick and their black clothing is not conducive to car avoidance.

The bus-victory has left a spring in my step and I am up the 12 steps in record time, too quick to have retrieved the keys from my pocket, and too quick to have noticed the big iron grille on the front door.

It is a beautiful iron grille. I'm not convinced that even with my arsenal of tools locked away within I could penetrate it. I had not thought outside the box. It would appear I have been out-secured. To her credit the idea is simple enough. I simply hadn't anticipated her being so childish, or so prompt. I hadn't expected her discovery to come for days yet, and even then I thought maybe she would accept defeat upon seeing the lengths that I had gone to.

I slide my back down the grille and sit in a puddle. I then have to sit on the urge to go inside to change my trousers. Wet-bummed, I check the date in my head. Yes it would appear my contract expired yesterday, or was it the day before? At any rate it has expired and my eviction is complete. I expected my eviction to be more emotional. I expected raised voices and the tearing of clothes. I had expected paperwork, threats, notice served, and legal mumbo-jumbo, but not this ornate and beautiful iron gate.

I have been deprived all that. This wet arse is hardly worthy of any memory space on the old hard drive.

When In Rome:

"I'll give you the guided tour," Gav says. Roughly translated this means he'll point out what I am not to touch and what bits the open invite does not extend to. This I freely accept, and I lift both corners of my mouth in preparation for expressions of awe at the fish tank I have heard far too much about.

After insisting I take my shoes off, which I do immediately in case they get dirty inside, Gav points out the bathroom on the right, which at a glance has a bath, sink, toilet an interesting array of porn on the cistern. Next, I'm ushered past his bedroom, which I am told is a mess and not worth smelling, into the front room, which he bizarrely calls the 'lounge', and points out the settee, which he pompously calls the 'couch'. This is to be my bed for the night.

The sofa, for it is indeed a sofa bed, has a rather good design. Whilst Gav is moving a four-pack of cider from the fridge to the freezer, I inspect the opening mechanism under the base. The mattress itself is sprung, on a metallic base supported by 24 individually sprung wooden slats. The front portion of the base has two oversize acrylic wheels to avoid undue carpet compression in anyone particular place when in either position. All round it is a very good piece of kit. I am going to be happy here. Gav returns with a couple of cans and plots down on one end of the sofa. I ask if I may jump in the shower quickly as I'm filthy and wet. He nods his head and remotes the TV into action. With great relief I realise that I am being ignored as though I have been here for weeks already. If there was a polar bear in here he would have just fallen through the ice.

I cannot comprehend the towel system. I'm able to see that there are three very distinct piles of towels; one near to the washing bin, one inside the bath, and one just inside the bathroom door. They are not divided by colour, size, or any other factor that I can discern from a distance. I go out on a limb and conclude that they must be sorted in order of cleanliness. The misleading pile near the washing bin I am almost certain are the clean towels waiting

Paul McMahon – Dead Reckoning

folding. This I deduce by touch as they are slightly abrasive in the way newly washed towels go without softener.

The other two piles are quite a mystery. I decide to tackle this problem under the shower and give it some serious thought, but the addition of scalding hot water to the conundrum doesn't have any positive effect, and I am left to drip dry in the corner.

It's too dark to see my watch, which I think is on a table. I can't remember, however, where this table is or any of the rest of the furniture for that matter. More worryingly, I can't recall where the light switch is. All things considered this might throw a spanner in the works of the toilet dash I am just about to embark on, having awoken in desperate need. My bladder has decided somewhere along the line that it doesn't need to seek permission for anything these days/nights. It conducts its own business at will, perhaps in revolt at being so overworked and unappreciated these last few years.

A river less travelled:

I am distressed getting dressed. Gav's up-late routine is unnatural to me and my loaned uniform does not fit. It is suffering from old age, its joints are worn, and there are the beginnings of a hole under the right arm. Not to seem ungrateful I leave the moaning until we have left the house.

I'm on edge this morning as I'm unfamiliar with the route to the bus stop, which appears out of nowhere all of a sudden. The people amassed here are all very alert and are staring at me. I panic at regular intervals as all my personal effects are in the wrong pockets, despite the trousers being of the same design as my own. I'm annoyed now as the bus is late. A few seconds pass and, alarmed, I turn to the timetable for support before I hear other passengers making pleased noises as the driver pulls up 'early'. In all this confusion I temporarily loose Gav in the bustle and begin to stress that I don't know which of the seats are lose, which side of the bus has the best view or exactly how long the journey should take. I am beginning to hyperventilate when I re-sight Gav some way back on the bottom level. Slowly I regain control by closing my eyes and humming some Miles Davis 'Doxy' to myself.

For whom the bell tolls:

I am trying to allocate blame for my recent detailing. It has been getting progressively worse of late, but it doesn't get any worse than a funeral escort. Not unless you happen to be white with a shaved head and the funeral in question is a Jamaican one held in the depths of East London. We will be like two white spots on a domino.

I phone the security department to check that it was not some sick joke, and to my horror it is confirmed. The Governor states, in a sadistically upbeat manner, that I should consider myself fortunate as he is letting me choose my own oppo. I ask him if I may take anybody, and he confirms this. I then ask him which wrist he wants handcuffed to the prisoner. He laughs as though I'm joking and walks off to his coffee machine and his buffalo leather chair with synchronised tilt mechanism, full five point seat adjustment, and tension control to adjust to individual body weight. I can feel my mood shifting. That buffoon isn't worthy of a chair like that. I feel myself getting angry as he hasn't even noticed that I adjusted his multi-adjustable armrests for width, height *and* angle. It must be so uncomfortable for him, but he hasn't the intelligence to do anything about it. A man like this in charge of a chair like that.

Paul McMahon – Dead Reckoning

I pick up the escort bag and phone the wing to arrange for the con to be collected and ferried over to reception. Gav answers the phone, and I tell him I have some bad news for him. I take great glee in stating that the Governor has ordered that we both have to go out. I spend the next few minutes explaining to Gav how to put in a Grievance against the Governor, for constructive bullying.

Gav is not happy at all and makes it clear to the inmate that this is how he feels. Everything is moving apace, and we are in the strip room in reception with BK7998 Brown, who has been smiling ever since Gav started to sound off on the way over. This smile, or smirk, appears not to have gone unnoticed by Gav, and I'm wondering how today is going to pan out when Gav slaps me hard round the face. I'm not sure who is more shocked, myself or Brown. I miss most of the next few seconds as I'm holding my ear, which is ringing. When I do look round I see Gav on top of a bewildered Brown, in direct contravention of PSO 1600, screaming something I assume must be "staff". I can't tell where the ringing in my head stops and the alarm bell I can hear begins. Not to look yellow, and as a sort of ingrained response, I too jump on Brown, who at this moment is lying on his back. In amongst all the flailing of limbs, I'm able to see that there is a distinct lack of smirk on his face.

Staff arrive promptly and I am relieved without any protest from me. I'm directed toward the medical room in Reception by two very concerned looking staff who are looking at the left side of my face. I can hear screaming coming from behind me, and thuds - Brown must be getting a good shoeing. I almost feel sorry for him.

I'm on my way out of the nurse's hatch when I am approached by an ashamed looking Gav. He pulls me to one side and apologises for the state of my face. Although I'm aware we

Paul McMahon – Dead Reckoning

have violated the establishment's decency agenda, I accept his apology with the good grace that a guest in somebody's house should do.

Glass houses/stones:

I break stride whilst walking down the road away from work as I'm surprised by a friendly female voice behind me informing me that I look like shit. Still continuing in the same direction, I turn around to apologise for offending her delicate eyes and realise, to my horror, that it's the nocturnal street junkie with whom I have unwittingly shared my garden and my hallway carpet. Not losing any momentum, I turn the 180 seamlessly into a 360 whilst flashing a smile, and leaving a wave for her behind me.

I don't want to risk increasing my speed, as that would look bad, so I just stare at the floor and hold out for the nearest bus stop.

I have never understood why women slip their arm through a man's whilst walking along. I can think of no other explanation than that it denotes ownership and, if that be true, what happens now is very bad news indeed.

She apologises to me, explaining that she can't walk too far with me as she has an appointment to keep, as if I had invited her along the pavement and will be heartbroken that she has to go.

Apparently she has been calling me all the way down the road; she had spotted me at work in the visits hall; couldn't believe it was me, and just wanted to say "Hi".

Paul McMahon – Dead Reckoning

Breakers ahead:

This knocks the wind out of my sails and I stop walking immediately. The fact that I'm in the middle of the road is not my main concern right now. My current grid reference is way down my list of things to worry about, most definitely below having a criminal woman know that I am a prison officer and know my address. The same cannot be said, however, for the transit driver I spot at the last second. He's probably got my grid reference at top spot of his agenda as he ploughs into me.

I had no idea how resilient the human body is. Granted I haven't been hit with any real force, just enough to knock the wind out of me a second time. As if I'm not concerned enough about being seen with a con's associate, I am now lying in the road with a crowd of people pointing and ooo-ing, and this cold-sored mess flapping around me, drawing all sorts of attention to me. To her. To us.

I roll over onto my front, and bring my knees up so that I am on all fours. It is at this point I realise my right hip is hurting and that I'm going to be unable to walk without the cause of all this mess. She comes around to my right side and aids my verticalness. That done, I insist that we leave as quickly as we can, or rather as quickly as I can, which isn't very quickly. I make an effort so as not be seen fraternising with a 'visitor'.

After a few steps she asks if I want to go to the hospital, which I do not. She then asks me if I can manage all those steps at my flat. I don't feel like explaining my homelessness to her at present, and Gav is working until late tonight, so I simply say that I won't be able to manage them.

She doesn't ask any further questions, just continues to prop me up and take the strain and, so subtlety that I don't even notice the change, take the lead and guide me very slowly down one side road then another, then an alleyway. I have my suspicions as to where we are going, but if she doesn't ask then I can't say no.

Home sweet home:

I am almost comfortable on this armchair. I have nearly discovered a position for my arse that doesn't encourage the renegade spring to come though the covering and pierce my rump. It has taken a little shuffling, the majority accomplished during her rinsing of my coffee mug, and the remainder I am now passing off as hip pain.

Even the smell isn't as bad as I had first thought, although I may have just become immune to it. As far as I can recall it was cat wee, but I can neither see nor hear any cats.

I'm looking around the front room of the flat trying to find pictures of family or friends that might contain the inmate she was visiting, but I can see none. I can see no photos, no posters, no wallpaper, nothing. None of the furniture matches, all of it either watermarked or scratched, as if each piece has been rescued from a skip, and the carpet is actually made up of around five or six rugs of varying shag and colour strewn across the floor. The coffee table is an old tea urn box turned on its side with an incongruous lace cover draped over the top. The only other objects to speak of are a television set and VCR on the floor in the corner with a West Ham FC video lying on the top, and a singular rubber plant next to the window, trying as best as it can to make a break for the light.

Paul McMahon – Dead Reckoning

The only things out of place in all this oddity are four brand new shiny laptop boxes in the corner of the room, presumably containing laptops of the rip-off variety.

My coffee is placed on the urn box in front of me, just out of reach. I spend the next minute or so trying to decide whether to let it go cold and un-drunk, or to ask for it to be passed to me, and risk looking like a lazy advantage-taking, piss-taking twat.

I tune in for a little while, waiting for a natural break in her monologue in which to butt in and deal with the coffee distance issue. It doesn't come very quickly. I ponder, while I should be listening, that there are two sorts of people in this world; those who actually have a conversation, and those that simply wait for their turn to speak. When there is a little break, I seize the moment:

Actual conversation No. 10:

Me: I don't suppose…

Her: Yes, of course…

Me: That was easy…

Her: I was waiting for you to ask…

Me: Ahh…I didn't want to be rude.

Her: It far ruder not to listen to somebody though innit?

Me: Yeah, sorry, it's the hip.

Her: Oh yeah, sorry.

Paul McMahon – Dead Reckoning

Me: Thanks for this.

Her: The coffee?

Me: Yeah, the coffee and letting me stay.

Her: You're welcome…Oh "stay"?

Me: Yeah, I mean…

Her: I didn't mean for you to stay, stay…

Me: Sorry, I thought…

Her: No I meant while you sorted your self…

Me: Of course…

Her: You know…

Me: That's what I meant…sorry…

(Pause)

Her: Obviously you can stay until then…

Me: Yeah.

Her: I mean…until you get somewhere else.

Me: Until I'm sorted?

Her: Of course…yeah…until then, then. Okay?

Me: Okay. Thank you….

Paul McMahon – Dead Reckoning

Her: Jackie.

Me: Thanks Jackie.

Jackie: You're welcome

I take a gulp of my coffee and nestle back a little further into the armchair. Jackie tells me to make myself... and then giggles, and explains she is going up to get changed. As she goes out of the front room I take the opportunity to phone work, after easing my phone gently out of my pocket, and tell Gav I won't be coming back to his for the night. I decide I ought not to tell him where I'm staying and tell him I'm stopping in hospital overnight and I will call him in the morning. Gav declares that news of my fight with a white van man is all over the prison. Being that it happened just down the road I should have expected nothing else. Gav tells me that the S/O knows and isn't expecting me in for a week, so to take as much time off as I need. I ask Gav to pass on my thanks and tell him I'll check in tomorrow.

Jackie comes back into the front room with wet hair. She tells me where the toilet is - being straight ahead at the top of the stairs - and asks me not to go in the room on the left. I don't ask why and she doesn't say.

<u>Self Medication:</u>

There is something very alluring about class As when you wake yourself up screaming in the middle of the night, having

Paul McMahon – Dead Reckoning

forgotten about your hip and stood up as per normal. The suggestion that I burn some skag with my new flat mate Jackie doesn't sound as ludicrous as it otherwise would do, minus the excruciating pain and lack of legal prescription pain killers.

I can say with a fair degree of certainty that this first hit has taken most of the edge off my hip. It has in fact taken most of the edge off everything. I reconcile my dipping my toes in the dirt river as being out of necessity and not out of desire. I doubt whether that will stand up to any clean scrutiny, but at the moment it is enough for me to forget about it and enjoy the buzz. I'll ruminate on it all later. Much later.

Two Stone(d) with one bird:

I have woken feeling sick - ashamed and sick right down to my very bowels. I want to retch this feeling of shame out of my system and cleanse myself. I've seen what this stuff does to souls and I am not about to hitch a lift on the smack express. I settle on the idea that the best way for me to repay Jackie's charity is to have her home raided by the police. Hopefully her arrest will solve both my problems in one fell swoop.

I have no idea how long she has been sitting there – it's pretty dark with the curtains drawn, and she is staring so intently at me that I wonder if I was thinking out loud. I guess "morning" at her, to which she giggles and shakes her head at me through her cigarette smoke. She tells me that she was just thinking about waking me up, as she has an appointment. Her client is arriving in ten minutes and she's going to need the front room.

Partly because I don't want to hole up in her bedroom, and partly because it's tipping it down outside, I ask her to cancel her

Paul McMahon – Dead Reckoning

appointment and propose that I compensate her for any sales she might make. This seems to please her quite a lot and she stands, retrieves her mobile and appears to send a pre-stored text message.

I'm wondering how much this is going to cost me as she walks over to where I am slouching, slips her dressing gown off her shoulders and lets it drop to the floor. I make a mental note than I need to improve my communication skills as she straddles me, for this is most definitely not what I meant.

I don't think that even a physiotherapist could have made this activity any less painless. Furthermore, her theatrical screams of supposed enjoyment are having the required effect and I reach climax before I can say "handling stolen goods." What a consummate professional she is. Her talents will be wasted inside - depending on which establishment she goes to. Caught up in the moment before I leave, I give her a quick Judas kiss. Cold sore or no cold sore.

30 pieces of silver:

I call the local police station and report that I have just heard screams coming from her apartment, which is true. I'm not a massive fan of lying if I can help it.

The sight line from this pub is not the best but the bar directly opposite doesn't do house doubles. Therefore, I make a decision to stay here in 'The Beachcomber' based on the fact that, if I am too close to the action, I may get caught up in this whole incident. I select a booth next to the window at the side of the pub, with Chesterfield-style padding, and stock up on a few pints of

Paul McMahon – Dead Reckoning

Guinness; the pints might have to stand a while, knowing London coppers, and lager just doesn't have the staying power.

I'm considering another trip to the bar, when a patrol car pulls up directly outside the block. Two very young PCs get out of the car, and don their hats before waddling over to the door. The taller of the two bangs on the door and they wait a while, laughing at something they have spotted around the door way. Some time passes and the smaller one takes his turn to bang on the door and prods away at the door bell for good measure.

Just as they're looking as if they might leave, the door opens. Jackie is standing in the door way in her dressing gown. There are about 30 seconds of talking, and a few shrugs of the shoulders by the smaller adolescent PC. Then the taller PC points into the flat. Jackie does not look too bothered from here, standing out of the way and ushering them in to get on with their Police business. The door shuts and I take the opportunity to head to the bar.

Restocked with a bottle of Gold Label and a can of nuts, I resume my position. Enough time passes that I actually begin to think Jackie has invited them in for some business of her own. Perhaps they were her earlier appointment and she just postponed them a while. Maybe they're regulars. I'm considering phoning the police corruption hotline I have stored in my mobile, when the door opens and Jackie is escorted to the police car. Walking in front is the very smug-looking tall PC and behind, carrying some boxes, the strutting smaller one.

Having nowhere else to go, and appreciating 'The Beachcomber's' décor, the efficient landlord and the sports channel, I visit the bar once again. There doesn't appear to be much in the way of passing trade on this road, as I've been pretty much the only person in here for the last few hours, and I've seen no more than two or three people walk past. The TV is on, but not really being interested in the report on the current sexual politics of the Austrian bobsleigh team, I turn my attention back to the street in time to see a group of muddy prepubescent boys kicking a ball between them as they approach from the other direction with overnight bags. One of them, in an old West Ham top, starts to skilfully juggle the ball with his feet as he breaks off over the other side of the street, before finally passing it back across the road and waving at his impressed and cheering friends. The lad fumbles around in his pockets as the others walk off, retrieves a set of keys and unlocks a door. Not just any door, but that door. Maybe that room wasn't full of sex dungeon bits or stolen power tools; maybe it is full of West Ham posters. I don't remember there being any other flats beyond that front door, just Jackie's. But then I wasn't looking. I probably got it wrong. Think about something else.

I ask the landlord if he has any rooms above the pub, which he states he does. This pleases me. He tells me that they are mostly let to people claiming asylum, and the rest through some sort of hostel, which I don't fully understand. This doesn't please me. He eyes me up and down, standing here in my black work trousers and white shirt, and appears to think for a second. He then says that the top level of a unit he owns down the road is a maisonette, and that he is looking to rent it out to a particular sort of a person. The rent is less than I was paying before and is closer to work, so I ask if I may take a look; he throws me a set of keys which are hung up behind the bar next to some old photo of a policeman with an Alsatian. Then he scrawls an address down on the back of a beer mat and slides it across the bar to me. I can't help thinking people are far too trusting.

Paul McMahon – Dead Reckoning

The entrance to the flat is out the back of 'The Beachcomber's' car park, and through the alleyway directly opposite. I make my way along it, and emerge outside the back of a large restaurant kitchen. My arrival is acknowledged by a grubby chef in checked trousers, puffing away on a roll-up outside his fly net doorway. I read the address to him and he points up above his head, then to a set of metal stairs diagonally behind me to my left which wind up and round to a doorway straight above where he is standing. As I reach the top I walk past the vents to the extractor fans below, blowing out a warm reassuring smell from the kitchen underfoot.

The flat is completely devoid of any furniture, so there is not that much to look at, but I am rather partial to a bit of seafood and, judging by the smell coming up through the floor, 'The Ocean Platter' doesn't do curry. The front door looks secure enough, and there is a fully functioning set of taps in each of the two rooms which should have them. There is an extremely long plasterboard wall that runs the full length of the flat from hallway through to the lounge, which doesn't have any of that annoying pebbledash wall paper that is hard to get a nice finish on when affixing cuttings over it. This will do me fine. After 'viewing' the flat I return down to the yard outside the kitchen area, where the chef is still puffing away on the same roll up. I introduce myself and we shake hands. I do not react to fact that his is wet, and maintain a firm grip and prolonged eye contact. That greeting went as well as can be expected. I ask him how long the flat has been empty and he shrugs his shoulders, and then says in broken English something that sounds like he doesn't know. Without prompting he then tells me he has been here three months, and that he supports Manchester United.

I return back to The Beachcomber to see the landlord, and tell him that I like the flat. He tells me that I can move in when I like. I tell him that I like right now. He smiles and tells me that as soon as I have paid the deposit then the keys are mine. This is a problem, and I tell him so. He again eyes me up and down studying

Paul McMahon – Dead Reckoning

my black trousers and white shirt. He spends a few seconds on my shoulders, pondering the loose flapping, epaulette lapels. Then he leans over the bar and looks at my black polished boots. This done he winks at me and says that I can pay at the end of the month, which is in a few days. There is evidently some kind of misunderstanding happening here that I am about to be the direct beneficiary of, and I am not going to clear it up if it means I can get my hands on these keys. So I wink back, and hold my hand out. I must get back to work, where I can be of some use, where I understand and am understood and there is some semblance of order.

Home is where the heart is:

Walking through the main gate at work feels as close as I have felt for days to a homecoming. The squeal of metal on metal hinges greets me at the first corner. Nothing has changed. I can hear the shouts from the windows, and I can feel my spine elongate and my muscles relax. I know the weight of every gate and can judge its closing to a millimetre. My keys feel warm in my pocket, and my keychain pats me comfortingly on my leg as I walk, full of purpose, out of the sterile area to the wing. I am acknowledged by all who pass, some breaking off conversations to ensure their hello lands. How I have missed and been missed.

Gollum on the desk is surprised to see me as I walk in, as is the Cleaning Off a little later and, later still, Gav, but none of them are as flabbergasted to see me as the S/O.

I am ushered into the office and offered the Talbot recliner, which I appreciate. The S/O shuts the door behind him and comes to perch on the desk uncomfortably close.

Paul McMahon – Dead Reckoning

Darwin himself would be proud of this story, as it seems to have taken on a life of its own, evolved, nigh mutated, in less than 48 hours into a distant ancestor of the truth. If I am to understand it correctly, I have pushed a little old lady out of the path of a crazed drunk driver in a bashed up old van, who then tried to reverse over my heaving near dead frame. Sensing that this may be a 1977 Reserve moment, I wince a little, shut my eyes at the disturbing memory, and nod my head.

When I open my eyes the S/O hasn't budged and is whiskey-less which perplexes me. I give myself a mental kick, and wonder if it's too late to mention that the driver was black. That would have nailed it, but it is too late and I don't want to jeopardise the kudos I've already snaffled. I've missed a trick there and will have to live with it.

The S/O insists that I'm on light duties until I am fully recovered; it's either that or I have to leave the prison. I accept, but ask if I can at least stay on the wing. We compromise, and he details me the front desk, much to the obvious annoyance of Gollum who is packed off upstairs to fend for himself amongst the cons.

Whilst I am going for a piss, I am mumbling something to myself in the staff toilet without realising it, and so Gav lets me know what a fucking retard I sound like when he undoes the cubicle door behind me and comes out laughing. He must have been in there for ages, as I've been standing here post-piss, cock in hand, in a world of my own for some time. Gav asks what I'm so het up about, and in an uncharacteristic display of openness I tell him straight away that I am broke and need to pay my deposit before the end of today. Gav looks genuinely upset that I'm struggling financially and immediately offers to pay it for me. I don't why I say no, because I desperately *want* him to pay it for me.

Paul McMahon – Dead Reckoning

Luckily, Gav insists which affords me the opportunity to feign reluctant acceptance. He tells me that he'll get the cash at lunch time, as he has to go out to his car anyway. I think what he means is that he can go to the cashpoint *in* his car, but I don't want to correct his grammar when he's being so nice to me.

Ship shape and Bristol fashion:

I am not going to let the front desk secretarial-style chair fuck with my mojo. Granted, it's not the Governor's chair, that is sat unused and unattainable behind a locked door, and which I'm sure has a fully synchronising mechanism with weight tension control, but I focus on its positive aspects. A quick appraisal reveals that it has a durable five-star base with twin wheel castors, gas seat adjustment and a hinged tilt backrest. I expertly heighten the chair and assume my position. I move the role book to the front of my work space then place the tools like stylograph, stapler and pencil, near me in order of their frequency of use. I switch the phone to my right side so the cord doesn't hang across my access route, and slide all the remaining crap onto a newspaper and banish it into the cupboard on my bottom left. I call a cleaner over to wipe the top section of the desk furthest away from me and give the front a quick polish. If this were my regular duty I would insist that all the muck be picked out of the screw heads in the woodwork, and that it were waxed and varnished like a figurehead.

The new Residential Governor enters the wing, and I stand barking out the wing roll, E-man count and 2052sh numbers. He looks a trifle astonished at my declaration and obviously isn't used to being displayed such respect. This I'm not surprised at, as it is alleged his last management position was at a supermarket, and his qualification for this high-ranking discipline service job amounts to nothing more than a degree, in accounting, from the University of Leicester.

The purser approaches the desk and begins to ask me questions. The difference, I feel, on this occasion is that this Governor is asking in earnest because he doesn't know the answers, and not because he is conducting some sort of covert on-the-spot job appraisal. I answer his questions truthfully, resisting the temptation to supply him with nonsensical figures and regulations in the hope he may regurgitate them and humiliate himself in the weekly management meeting. I understand the pecking order, and respect his position.

He is pleased with our exchange and, when directed by me, heads towards the door to the captain's office. I decide it best that the purser-governor learn from his own mistake on this occasion, and I don't warn him to knock. The S/O hates being barged in on. The screaming starts just as the door closes and I pity the purser-governor for a few seconds, until I remind myself of his pay packet and the gas powered swivel chair he inherited with his new office.

A shot across the bows:

I grab the application box and tip all the requests to see the S/O into the bin in front of a massive queue of prisoners. When asked 'what the hell' I'm doing I explain that the S/O is there for officers and not prisoners, and advise the chap nearest the desk to Fuck off, which he does accommodatingly.

Paul McMahon – Dead Reckoning

Some of the old faces clear away from the desk, taking some of the well-liked new faces with them. The more time served behind a door the more sensitive to changes in the commune's mood one becomes; some of the old school cons are better at sensing trouble than meerkats or bees, and are just as quick to disperse. This leaves about three or four street rats within the immediate area of my desk that are not astute enough to pick up on the rather large hint I have dished out. One of the creatures walks up to the desk as if he has a stone in one shoe, and has the audacity to perch his rear end on it. I advise him to get the fuck off my desk, without looking up from the role book. He does as instructed, but then leans his hands on the desk, stooping down to speak to me. I do not like having to repeat myself, so I knock both his wrists out from under him and slam his head into the desk. I love the smell of alarm in the morning. For reasons best known to themselves the two remaining rats disappear; maybe they were missing the start of Jeremy Kyle or their problems had simply resolved themselves, I do not know. Bar a few whimpers from out of sight, I note a certain tranquillity has descended upon the bottom landing, and I am sure I see a tumbleweed blow by.

Happy as a clam at high tide:

I'm in good spirits. I am also in a very good mood indeed after discovering them. As well as an antique mouse trap and a wok, the last tenants have left a bottle of Metaxas brandy and I am just sampling one or two glasses. Surfing on the back of this rare good fortune I decide to see what effect my good mood has on John.

I can hear seagulls somewhere out of sight. I'm not sure what they're doing this far inland but I prefer their company than to that of the pigeons that plague this city. I take the long way round to 'The Beachcomber', as I'm not sure if I was rude to 'Fat Cook' last night. Coming out onto the edge of the common, I

Paul McMahon – Dead Reckoning

pause and stare out over the heath admiring the ravens as they patrol their sacred site. I admire the peculiar people with their kites rallying against gravity and pitching battle against the elements. A pursuit with no end gain, but oh my, what fruitless fun it looks.

John the Landlord is pouring my chosen tipple as soon as I walk through the door of the pub. This always makes me feel special. I pull up my stool at my end of the bar and line up my cigarettes, lighter and shrapnel in front of me. When I look up, a middle-aged black chap in a wax jacket is paying for my pint, which he is taking a sup out of. I am trying to place his face when John looks over and asks me what I'm having. He knows what I'm having. The Waxman thanks the "Gov'nor" in a broad cockney accent, throws his rifle range in his sky rocket, and wobbles off with his Shaun Ryder. I opt for a wife beater, throwing a little curve ball, forcing John to change the glass he has already picked up for me, which makes me chuckle and maintains my good mood. I allow myself a little eyeballing of the cheeky Waxman getting Schindler's-List in the corner.

I turn my attention to John who is staring out of the window trying to visually intimidate people into his pub. It is not working. He is pushing his I-hate-the-world character to a whole new level today, and by the look on his mush I get the impression that business must be pretty bad. He will most definitely be grateful for the extra income from my rent. Remembering that I have Gav's money in my pocket, I slide the envelope over the bar to him. John takes the envelope off the bar and puts it in the till without counting it. He says thanks, although due to his current mood it doesn't actually come across as thanks, more "I could snap at any second". I mull over a few conversation starters - like the plight of real ale, the smoking ban, and the Fat Cook - before thinking better of it and sliding the remainder of my pint down my gullet. No sooner have I placed the empty pint pot on the jump than John has started pouring me another, without asking. I had intended to inflict my joviality on the rest of the world but Angry-John has

Paul McMahon – Dead Reckoning

other ideas. I thank him, and offer him a pint hoping that this will oil the wheels for some banter. He thanks me, dead pan, without breaking his gaze from the window, and tells me that he is grateful and will leave it in the tap for later. In effect I have just been mugged off, but remarkably my mood has remained intact.

This time I stand and don my jacket while my pint is still half full. I give further indication of my intention to leave by putting my belongings in my pockets, before downing the rest of my lager in one. I thank Angry-John, and nip into the toilet to evacuate my bladder before I hit the cold air; which is fortunate, as I piss like a race horse for a full minute.

Having had my constitutional and not wanting to waste my positive frame of mind, I make a snap decision to retrieve my possessions from Mrs Porter. I am on the bus immediately, albeit the wrong one, but there is nothing like living in the moment.

Omnia mea mecum porto:

On arriving at the yard door, I can hear voices calling to each other in some Eastern European dialect, and the two-tone whirring from some power tool. I approach, stick my head round the door, and see one man hanging a new front door on the bottom flat, while two more young men are cutting what appears to be a worktop surface down to size with a circular saw. There is a small transistor radio playing in the background, and a fourth man is singing along to an Oasis song in broken English, while he carries a toilet cistern up the steps to my old flat.

Upon seeing me, the older man dealing with the door downs his tool and greets me. He only speaks enough English to explain to me that he doesn't speak English, and then he shrugs his shoulder and points at me in an effort to ask me what it is that I want. The other two young workers are not interested in my presence whatsoever, and carry on shouting at each other over the sound of the saw, with the one weighing the work surface down at one end doing most of the hollering.

I point at myself and then upstairs to the flat. He stares blankly at me, waiting for me to finish the thought. I stare at him thinking there is no full stop in charades. Sensing that a few props might help, I draw my keys out from my pocket and rattle them at him. He nods his head and widens his eyes, pointing at all of the new fixtures lying around in polythene on the yard floor. I shake my head and wave my hands over each other. This is harder than I thought it might be. I pick up an old lampshade that is lying to my right and point at it. He seems to understand what I am talking about and laughs, melodramatically slapping himself on the knees with both hands. As he stands, he points back over his shoulder, and gives me the thumbs up. Ok, so now we're getting somewhere.

He lights up a cigarette, pats me on the shoulder and walks out through the door in the direction of the road. Just outside there is a tarpaulin, which he whips back, exposing a pile of clothes and CDs. There are also a few bin liners with slits in them where the odd picture frame or piece of cutlery is poking through. I thank my new friend and pull a £20 note out of my wallet, offering it to him, which he accepts with a smile, and goes back to his work. I had not expected there to be anything left. I had also not actually expected him to take the money, I was just being nice. This trip has been worth it. I sort through what's there and siphon off about two bin bags of stuff I decide I can't really do without, and leave the rest where it is. As I am doing up the last bin bag, I catch sight of My Armchair. Some of My Armchair. Or rather, a piece of My Armchair. It has been broken down into segments so that it doesn't take up too much space in the skip. The material is ripped and it is completely beyond repair. I am suddenly overcome with nostalgia.

Paul McMahon – Dead Reckoning

I'm hit with a real sense of sentiment, and for the first time feel loss.

Saturated Market:

You can get drugs anywhere. I am convinced that if I were dumped naked in a field in the middle of nowhere, with nothing but a 20 pence piece taped to my back, that I could still be off my nut by lunchtime. I walk down the pavement away from the flat as aggressively as my hip will allow, which is surprisingly aggressively, in the direction of the hostel on the common. As I approach, I can see two scruffy 'oiks sat on the wall at the front. The closer of the two is sizing me up, presumably deliberating whether he will have more luck with the spare fag or spare change ploy. He wisely picks the former, and is as surprised as I am when I stop and offer him one.

Poking out of his mandatory blue carrier bag, I can see some distinctive purple cans. In the spirit of trade, I offer him the remainder of the packet for a tin of brew. I'm aware that I may have been too generous here, but it's saved me a walk and I'm about as concerned about the finer economics of the deal, as I am about the temperature of the can. I console myself that the warmer the can, the easier to down, which is fortunate really as this tastes like shit. Resisting the urge to purge, I subdue the bile building and hold my breath. The Samaritan nearest me chuckles, sighs a knowing sigh, and offers me another.

I've been sat on this wall some time. My watch can't be more specific as it's dripping down my wrist, and my hands have lost their rigidity. My two friends are bilingual and my homing beacon is on the blink. At a loss I follow the blue bag inside the Georgian doors into a common room occupied by common people, one of which I sit on. They skip and jump from tangent to non sequitur and I appreciate their shoes.

My little doze has done me well. I think it's lucky that I'm so heavy as I've been sitting on my wallet, and they look to me like the sort who would have snaffled it if they had the opportunity - and had I not looked like somebody who wouldn't own one. Most people in the room are snoozing so I'm careful not to wake anybody as I leave, or as I edge an unopened can from a sleeping grip. I smell deeply of homelessness and can't wait to get in for a shower.

Lost in translation:

I wake up extremely hungry, on the one piece of furniture I now have in the front room. Although this pink chaise lounge looks utterly ridiculous in here, it is very comfortable indeed and well worth the embarrassment of carrying it down the road, in uniform, aloft my head. At the request of my belly, I hotfoot it in the ferocious summer sun, barefoot down the searing hot metal steps toward the restaurant's back door below. At first I just think the Fat Latvian Chef is just being rude. I've come into his kitchen many times before via the fly-net draped backdoor below my flat, and he has not minded one bit. He has on occasion even shared a can with me, in exchange for a cheeky mini-takeaway request, so I mistakenly think that he must just have a lot of orders on and is taking his stressful job out on me - until I catch a reflection of myself in the oven glass. In my defence, the whole flat move has been disorientating; the Armchair discovery hit me hard, and I'm not completely sure whether I'm coming or going. That said, I fully appreciate that kitchens have to comply with Environmental Health Laws, & Health and Safety Legislation, so even though I have had a bath, I accept the inference that inspectors would take umbrage over my body's second most hairy part not wearing a hair net. It is

Paul McMahon – Dead Reckoning

summer and still hot, so it's not uncommon for men to be topless. I know I'm topless. I didn't know I was also bottomless, and it's the bottom half that the problem. When half cut and hungry, it is an easy mistake to make. The Fat Latvian Chef is shouting at me and waving his knife around the other side of the hotplate, starring at my sausage meat like it might just be the next thing on the menu.

John the Landlord takes all this rather well, I think. It's hard to distinguish, through all his loathing for the world, which of his feelings of disgust and disappointment are aimed solely at me. He is pretty civil about the nakedness issue. He assures me he's seen a lot of cock in his time as a policeman. I feel this revelation regards his former employment explains a lot about his temperament - he is one bitter bastard. He explains that he has to keep in with the restaurant due to certain illegal building infractions that they are aware of, owing to the fact their properties adjoin each other. He explains that the chef, being Latvian, is an Orthodox Christian and that my sort of overt and unsolicited show of fondness is not acceptable in his country. There is no point challenging John about my sexuality, as he has already seen the Pink Chaise. He tells me he has been round to clear out the flat this morning, after I had gone to work. I ask him for my clothes, which he produces straight away from under the bar, hoisting them up whilst enlightening me about the extent of my bar tab. The bar tab comprises my bar tab as standard, and then my outstanding rent - the total of which I can't pay. John has already come to terms with this it seems, as he smiles and tells me that deposits were invented for this reason. I smile at him and hold my hands up. Fair cop.

NHS Bedlam/Non compus mentis:

The homeless hostel is charging £8 pounds a night apparently, according to homeless Melvin, the oracle at the entrance to the tube, who had to shut his eyes to tell me. However,

I do not feel adequately street-qualified to acquire this sort of cash at my first begging session, with or without Mervin as a mentor.

I recall a snippet of banter in the tea room at work about the nut house round the corner. I remember a fat, white nurse with alopecia and an Eastern European accent, saying something about it being like the Hilton; she'd done some agency shifts, money-grabbing, despite her union forbidding it. At a loss for any other ideas I begin to walk round the corner, toward the street in question.

The Mental Health Act 1983 seems to be far more complex than I could ever have imagined. I have booked in at the reception as an informal patient, having just walked off the street and declared that I am feeling peculiar and need somewhere to protect me from myself for a little while.

The whole process of checking in as an informal patient has been remarkably stress-free. As I am scanning through some laminated information pages in the drawer next to the bed where the bible should be, I wonder why backpackers and hobos the nation over have not picked up on this trick.

My ponderings are interrupted by Section 5, and I begin to think that this may not have been such a good idea after all. Section 5.4 relates to being 'detained' as a FORMAL patient at the *discretion* of the staff, specifically a nurse, one of whom I have just insulted, up to a maximum of six hours. My feelings are further compounded when I immediately try to check out and the nurse in question explains to me, with a dry smirk, that leaving during darkness is not permitted for reasons I do not fully understand. I stutter a little; she retorts before her turn that "rules are rules", turns on her pink Crocs and saunters off wiggling her perfectly formed rear end.

Paul McMahon – Dead Reckoning

Daylight +6hrs = A missed shift. I point this out to the rapidly departing nurse who calmly informs me of my shift's irrelevancy. She would make a great screw. That, and a great officer.

The walls are painted obligatory magnolia, although the eccentric singing toff I can hear down the hall may think them eggshell, or Egyptian cotton. In my room the interior designer/psychologist has chosen to display a Van Gogh painting. I can't help but think this is a little ironic considering he was so unbalanced from Absinthe that he cut his own ear off. Through boredom, I playfully spend a few minutes trying to dream up an angle with which to sue for mental cruelty, before I accept what a ludicrous claim it would be and imagine myself explaining to the judge that a painting made me do it. This makes me laugh out loud just in time for the nurse to walk in and, in the clear absence of a TV, radio, or any other stimulation in the room, concludes that I may very well be a madman after all.

It is the trying to act sober that gives away the drunk. In the same way my attempting to act sane is making me look anything but. My grandiloquent use of long words when talking to the nurse, in an attempt to accentuate my intellect, is not working in a good way. It is making me seem very odd indeed, and after allowing myself a scary irrational moment where I consider the prospect of never being allowed out again, I decide to come clean.

I explain about the flat, and Nick, and homeless Mervin, who seems to feature in my explanation rather more than he should for what in reality is just a cameo in my life. I explain about the drinking, and work, and make a point to emphasise its stresses using carefully selected synonyms such as 'pressure', 'tension', 'hassle', etc. I wonder if my ability to operate in such a taxing environment is impressing her as my eyes slide downwards, past her name badge which reads "Dymphna", along her necklace to her

Paul McMahon – Dead Reckoning

breasts. She listens attentively and then pauses, allowing the dust to settle on my outburst, and the tranquil balance to be resumed. Then she speaks.

What I don't like at all is having the tables turned on me. So when the nurse, after listening with complete serenity, tells me that by just choosing to walk into this building has been me subconsciously seeking help, I take it very badly.

I am very well aware that it is very mild at night this time of year, that even Melvin doesn't sleep swathed in newspaper. I know full well that there is a perfectly good bus depot round the corner, and that the warm 24 hour night buses run a regular service round London. I even know that the nearest hospital has a 24 hour casualty department, and if you push the reject button on the coffee machine half way through the dispensing your get your money back! I am perfectly well aware of the options in this area for the temporarily homeless but I happened to chance into this establishment…on a whim…there was certainly no rational thought behind it, and most definitely not a choice to surrender myself here, subconscious or otherwise. I never knew nurse's basic training covered the inner workings of the psyché. What an infuriatingly astute bitch.

I am almost too angry to speak but as it is my turn I find myself shouting at her that she is utterly gorgeous. It appears we are as confused as each other at this announcement, as there is another dust-settling pause. I suppose a psychologist may call this a masterful distraction technique as my apparent emotional surrender to Florence-fucking-nightingale here is not currently at centre stage.

If she is shocked, then she doesn't show it. She smiles a peaceful understanding smile, and asks me if I wish to rest now. Her tight fitting white uniform at this angle looks a little like a nun's habit. I expect the pendant at the end of her silver chain is a cross and that she will pray for my deviant soul the first opportunity she gets. I lay down on the bed just to test it.

The sun is so bright I think my eyes are already open before I open them. I must be late for work as I can smell cabbage, and nobody has cabbage for breakfast. At reception I sign what I can only presume are disclaimers, and walk out the front door with more purpose that a man with no abode is entitled to.

Dry-docked:

The only AA meeting I can find that's running today is being held at a community hall underneath a church. It looks an innocuous enough place from the outside. There is a fleur de lis on the outside of the door and I wonder if scouts or fascists are preordained to be alcoholics. I stand at the corner of the street, just far enough away smoking a cigarette. I'm nonchalantly trying to look distant and otherwise engaged, but with the entrance in my peripheral vision, waiting for my moment to slither inside invisible to all these nosy passers-by.

I sense a gap but procrastinate as my cigarette is only half finished. There will be other opportunities; if not today then next week, month, or year, in which to make another dash for it. Fag finished there is nothing passing save a metaphorical tumbleweed, and I reluctantly lollop over to the doorway.

The stairs are not well lit. There is a low hub-bub of people below and I edge through the bottom door paying particular attention to the carpet. There are approximately fifteen people standing on the carpet. There are plastic chairs with metal legs, the sort that are indigenous to schools, and a table in the left hand corner of the room, also standing on the carpet, upon which stands a tea urn. No one pays any attention to my entrance which is good. To avoid sticking out like an alcoholic I make my way over to the urn, where I take a polystyrene cup as a prop and hope I have slotted right in.

I am greeted by a man in shorts with muddy knees who smells of gardening. He stretches out a hand in my direction, which I instinctively take hold of and shake, realising too late his hand is shaped in a pointing gesture, and he was indicating the tea bags behind me. This is a source of much amusement to him, and a source of much embarrassment for me. I wonder if this could be going any worse.

'Muddy Knees' goes through the motions, introducing himself as Con and mechanically asking me how long it has been since my last drink. My answer makes Con choke on his tea, and I begin to feel there may be rules of membership to this club. Con rubs my back in a strangely familiar way, praises me for choosing the 'holistic route' whatever that is, and walks me over to the ring of chairs. People are beginning to assemble and Con nods at me to sit down as he does likewise to my immediate left. Out the corner of my eye I see Con motion to a man, hovering over the only wood and fabric chair, that I am new.

The wood and fabric man is about forty years old with light grey hair, a wide smile - the sort which is carried by the smug few who know something you don't know - and a pair of rectangular glasses, which he pushes back up his nose in readiness to speak. A general hush falls across the room. This man must be the leader of the sect.

The head honcho introduces himself as Robert or "Bob", welcomes everybody, and asks that if there is anybody that is new and wishes to make themselves known, then this is the time to do so. As everybody is already looking at me I don't see this is necessary, but I dutifully say hello and clarify to everybody who has

Paul McMahon – Dead Reckoning

never seen me here before, that I have never been here before. Everybody simultaneously welcomes me in chorus using my name and applauds me like I am Enoch Powell after the 'Rivers of Blood' speech.

Robert then throws the meeting open to the floor and there is a silence as a lot of very polite people offer each other their place in the queue, exchanging deferential glances and hand gestures toward each other.

40 days and 40 nights:

Someone from across the circle starts to speak. A long, thin man wearing tight cycling shorts which squeeze out of him a long, thin voice.

"I went walking the other day in Wales. I went walking and breathing. I spent some time amongst megalithic stones and inside nature. I tried to live inside every breath and cleanse my soul. I tried to focus on each breath and remember just how cold and clean each one was. I tried to focus on the air on my skin and the colours around me. The temperature, the wind, I tried to soak up everything that I could in each moment and really tune in to what it is like to be alive; to feel what it is like to feel. I remembered what it was like to not feel. To think of nothing, to be out of sync with the world and not care. To be out of key with nature. I try and get up to the hills once a year at this time. It strengthens my resolve. It reminds me of everything that I can't explain, and everything that I didn't know I'd forgotten."

Ship of fools:

I have no fucking idea what is going on here. Cycling Hippy has evidently swapped one vice for another as far as I am concerned and he is tripping on some high quality weed. There is much nodding and grunts of appreciation round the circle, like I missed out on the hash brownies. Even the man next to Robert who's head is fully covered in tattoos and probably had trouble understanding some of those long words, has his eyes closed, is sucking in deep breaths and looks like he is actually there in the valleys with him.

Hippy finishes speaking and there is a comfortable silence as people around me are invited to reflect by 'bob' on what has been "offered" by Hippy. After some time a younger girl, three people to my right, speaks quietly to the group. She explains that it is her turn to lead the group in meditation and asks us all to close our collective eye.

Abandon ship

I am invited to imagine that I am sitting at the bottom of the sea, that all sound is dulled and everything is slow and calm. I do not RSVP. I am asked to imagine, when I am ready, a bubble come up from the sand below me and gently make its way up in front of my eyes. I am in a state of unreadyness. I am asked to focus on the bubble and allow a word to enter it. Monotone advises me that if a word does not come freely, allow the bubble to go on its way and await the arrival of another bubble. I open my eyes and cast them around the circle. Everybody is so engrossed with their own self-indulgence, that nobody sees me leave.

Paul McMahon – Dead Reckoning

Revelation: P(int) art 6

I am watching a few solitary bubbles float up from the bottom of my glass in a pub called 'The Compass' down the road from the church. I don't really want to be here, but I can't not try out the high-backed, solid beech framed, Swanson bar stools that can be seen from the street outside. I love the rare arm rests on this stool, as they come in handy towards the end of a session. I'm shuffling my arse around on the embossed veneer seat in appreciation as 'Tattoo Man' walks in. He says nothing to me but nods a knowing nod, and slips into the bustle beyond. Busted.

It's raining so I don't mind pissing in my jeans so much as I would otherwise. The fresh air has hit me hard and I should have paid a final trip to the loos before I left the bar, but no matter – no-one will notice in this weather. The warm feeling is so pleasurable I almost miss the vibration of my mobile phone in my pocket. The voice on the other end has a somewhat sobering effect as my S/O tells me that Gav has been badly assaulted and is in hospital. He asks me if I will make my way there, as there is no-one listed on his next of kin details held in personnel.

Breakers yard:

After sleeping off the worst of it in the end cubicle of A&E, I have a thorough wash and head to the main desk. Subsequently I am directed to the lifts, holding a Post-It note with the ward I want written on it. On arrival, and chewing four Polo mints, I make my way to the nurses' desk and ask if I may see Gav. I may not, but I may see 'Gavin'.

Paul McMahon – Dead Reckoning

Gav's head looks like a big blister. His eyes have all but retreated inside his head so just two little Chinese slits remain. His nose is hardly any further forward than the rest of his puffy flesh, and he has Richard Prior lips. I take a snapshot for prosperity while the nurse is retrieving his possessions, just in case he is ever able to laugh about it in the future, which I doubt.

I show my ID and explain that Gav has no Family, which I am not sure about but take the house keys all the same. I make a list of things that the nurse advises me of:

Toiletries

PJ's

A book

Mobile phone

Et tu Brute:

Gav must have been in the middle of making a cake. There are a set of digital scales, a roll of cling film, and flour all over the worktop. I toss the keys down on top of some Tupperware and have a good look around. From the other room I can hear the repetitive bleeping of an alarm clock, muffled behind the bedroom door. I put myself to use tidying up the kitchen, so Gav won't have to do it when he comes home, and switch on the radio while I set to work breaking down the cardboard box of "Glucose Plus" sitting next to the bin. The annoying alarm is distracting me from the rhythmic genius of Phil Collins, so I head for the bedroom to stop it before he really gets going.

On Gav's bed side table there are three mobile phones. One of them is flashing to indicate an incoming call but is on silent. Next to the three phones is a pager sitting abreast a pile of bank notes one of which is rolled up. Next to this is a small velvet wallet, splayed open showing off its fancy little stitched partitions inside, poking out of which are a small mirror, old-fashioned razor blade and some kind of tiny glass vial containing something that I hope very much is milk powder.

I know I have been standing here a long time as Phil Collins and Chester's drumming duet, which has to have gone down in history as the longest drumming instrumental ever, has finished.

Just the one Mrs Wembley:

Of course I can't get angry without ascertaining if it is actually what it is, or rather what I think it is, that is, what I believe it to be. So I do.

I feel awakened and focused within seconds.

My heart is racing and my mind is dancing with pin point precision

Paul McMahon – Dead Reckoning

from one --
---clear idea -----------------------
----
to the next.

It suddenly seems so simple -------------------------------------
--and   I
whoop.

I actually whoop--
------ out loud.

I only now realise just how incredible Patti Smith ------------
----

----------------------------is.

how insightful a song this --------------------------------------
----
----------------------------is.

Paul McMahon – Dead Reckoning

I sit up straight and allow this dawning epiphany to wash over me and I understand in this moment, how righteous and just a course of action can truly be.

On closer inspection of the kitchen apparatus, I notice that the Tupperware containers all have little labels on the front. One of the labels reads 'H'. As much as I want to, all the evidence which surrounds me is making it very difficult for me to believe that this 'H' could reasonably stand for 'Hungarian Goulash'.

Breaking the Amalfitan code:

Inside the Tupperware is about a dessertspoon-sized amount of 'H'. It is an off-white colour and looks pretty innocuous just sitting there on the worktop. If it wasn't for the scales, phones, pager, and razor blades all over the place, it would just look like something I might use to sweeten my coffee. I pull up a stool and sit at the worktop for a little while, staring at it, trying to imagine what set of circumstances could have arisen that would make Gav do such a thing, to betray all of us. I can't think of a single scenario that would make me do it. I hate drugs. Not the drugs themselves really, but the fights, the debts, the heartache that comes with the whole package. I hate heroin.

Heroin slows down your mind and your body. Medically speaking it slows down your respiratory system. I've picked up a little knowledge on the subject speaking to junkies and nurses over the years. Even if you're not interested, you inadvertently become quite an authority on many scummy issues doing this job. I also know, therefore, that the worst thing you can mix heroin with is anything else that also slows down the respiratory system, such as a tranquiliser. We call these 'Benzo's at work - Benzodiazepines. The basic logic being that if you slow down something enough, eventually it stops, and if your respiratory system stops, meaning you stop breathing, then you stop. Living. This is nothing more than you deserve if you start fucking around with Junk. Like I always say, it's a one-way street.

It doesn't take me very long to find what I'm looking for. Gav has a few boxes of both Tamazipam and Diazepam in his bathroom cabinet which I'm looking at now. These tablets are issued for anxiety and stress. Poor fucker had a lot to be stressed about I suppose. I pop open the blister packs into a Mortar that Gav has lying on the kitchen worktop, and start to work the little tablets around with the pestle, round and round into a fine powder. I have a little look around the kitchen for anything I can use to alter the colour back, as it really should be a little browner. I find the spice rack and select a little nutmeg, which I sprinkle in sparingly so there is just a faint tinge. I want to hammer the point home, whatever my point is, so just to be on the safe side I add a little bleach powder from under the sink. Tasty. I don't really know why I'm doing what I'm doing. I could call the police, but I'm not going to, perhaps out of loyalty. I suppose I am doing this to take a few junkies out of the game, to stop Gav dealing by eliminating his customers. It sounds stupid now I think about it, reckless. I really don't know why I do anything, but it just feels right.

The mixture looks pretty good. I am unable to tell any real difference in texture and colour than the original mixture. I pour it all back into the Tupperware and replace everything back where it was. I collect Gavs overnight bag and leave for the hospital to play the dutiful friend, nursing a comforting tingle at the back of my throat.

Paul McMahon – Dead Reckoning

Hospital:

Gav is sitting up when I go through the door. After saying hello, he maintains eye contact with me for a moment too long, trying to gauge my face. I slip in early on that I haven't been in his bedroom by apologising for missing most of what was asked for by the nurse, as I had to be quick and I knew the fags were kept in the hallway drawer.

I ask Gav what happened to him. He tells me that he can't remember much past seven balling one of the cleaners on the pool table and winning a Mars bar. He explains that he was standing on the landing and must have been done from behind as he has no idea what he was hit with. I run out of things to say, and Gav goes quiet too. There is an awkward pause. Evidently programmed with a social etiquette setting, Gav's machines sense the tumbleweed and politely come to life and bleep away the silence. The rhythmic pulsing of the machine speeds up ever so slightly, and taking solace in Gav's discomfort, I close my eyes. The bleeping sounds like the emergency cell bells at work, and have a similar effect on my consciousness.

I awake to an African nurse barging into me with a blood pressure pump. Gav's head is pointing toward me. It's really anyone's guess as to whether he is awake; as his eyes are so swollen there really isn't any difference between their resting and attentive positions. I want to tell Gav about my dream seeing as he had a posthumous starring role. It was set around his gravestone which the POA had kindly adorned with a headstone saying, "A brave man". I suppose he must have had a set of balls to walk in the prison every other day with an arse stuffed with narcotics.

Gav is receiving much more attention that I expect an NHS patient to. The nurse with no special awareness moves to expose another petite South East Asian nurse on the other side of the bed, who is doing things to Gav's arm and shouting loudly. I want to tell her to be quite and have some respect and explain that she is in an English hospital, but I expect this information is already clearly marked on her pay slip.

Her shouty ways have alerted a very English-looking Doctor who has no doubt burst in to tell her to stick a sack of rice in it. It's only when he enters into a decibel-duet with her that I sense I may have misread the situation. It is like a scene off the television; each of the assembled medical practitioners is attempting to outdo each other with multisyllabled words, while hastily moving equipment around in an elaborate mechanical dance. I obligingly fall into my role and offer paltry "Somebody help him". This precipitates an early bath for me, as I am ushered out by the rugby sized nurse.

Standing outside the room where Gav is being massaged, I stare around at the other occupants of the corridor. The passage is filled by distraught people. Presumably their relatives have not been trafficking drugs into one of Her Majesty's prisons and do not deserve to die. I turn back to the nurses working away on the smuggling vessel, and wonder why they care so much.

The good thing about Gav being on his death bed is that that the nurses seem willing to bend the rules on non-immediate family sleeping in the relatives room. I plot myself down on the Z-bed, and switch on the TV/DVD combo. The nurse tells me that she will let me know the minute there is any development. I wish she wouldn't, as I'm exhausted and my hangover is beginning to kick in before I have even got to sleep; however, I have enough emotive savvy to realise this attitude may compromise my stay in the close relative suite.

I awake in exactly the same position that I went to sleep in, which tells me I needed the sleep. I doubt whether there really was enough space on the Z-bed to navigate a rollover anyway. But beggars can't be choosers, unless you're Melvin, in which case your income would enable you to live a frugal middle-class existence, presupposing you didn't have a habit, which he does.

I digress so far I can't remember what I am doing in this room anyway. I should probably get some rest. After all, I need to conserve my energy to support Gav.

A rude awakening:

Bull-in-a-chin- shop nurse fractures my sleepy ruminating by bursting in and making me flinch all too quickly for the Z-bed, resulting in a snap mattress cocoon.

Oddly for a caring profession, this Nurse seems to have no sense of humanity as she does not immediately come to my aid. Neither does she amble to my aid in a nonchalant fashion. In fact there is no aid forthcoming, willing or otherwise. Moreover this woman appears to have no sense of humour, as the sight of this newly podded visitor does not so much as raise a smile. Not that a smile would have been appropriate. In actual fact, should she laugh, or indeed so much as twitch with glee, I would, - not withstanding my padded restraints - attack her without hesitation, such is my rising embarrassment and the clinging grudge I have against her for having woken me rudely for the second time in as many seven o' clocks.

Hoist the Black Flag:

The fat stony faced African 'nurse' tells me that Gav died at 06:13hrs this morning. I don't hear the next part as I am distracted by her unwillingness to round it up to quarter past. Bizarrely, she asks if there is anything she can do for me, and more bizarrely, I don't ask her to help me out of my flytrap.

The nurse leaves and I am left comforted by the warm hug of the Z-bed.

There is always an excuse for a beer. Put me in any situation and I could engineer a reason why it is suitable – nay, wise - to consume a tipple. This situation, for instance, takes little ingenuity for justification; deaths and births are traditionally celebrated with a beverage of some kind. Think of something else.

I've passed three drinking holes on route to this boozer. This is not a good time to be risking new bar stools and fabric on the booths. This is a time for the familiar solid beech upholstered bar stools that I remember from getting sloshed in 'The Compass' after my disastrous AA meeting.

I time my arrival at the doors of 'The Compass' for opening time. I refuse to be one of those wankers waiting outside in a cue at the doors. I would much prefer to be the sort of wanker who waits in another location, preferably still in view so I don't waste that much time, and can still be one of the first to the bar.

Paul McMahon – Dead Reckoning

The doors are open and I start to fish around in my change pocket for pint and chaser shaped coins.

Fata morgana:

On entry I see that there is only one other person in 'The Compass'. He has sunk a pint of Guinness already and is staring away toward the opposite end of the bar from me, glass in hand, awaiting the arrival of the topper-upper. He attempts to hasten the speed of service by shouting "landlord" in a thick Irish drawl. I busy myself with seat selection, and choose one well-worn, high, wooden spindle-backed stool near the door, in which I sit and begin to arrange my coins on the bar top. I am making the last pile symmetrical when a pint of ale is placed before me. This is what I would have ordered anyway, although I think it a little presumptuous. No mind; I raise a little cash pyramid to the bartender, who holds out his hand at me like he is stopping traffic and points to the solitary Irish figure at the end of the bar.

Actual conversation No. 11:

Tattoo: Man: Going to the meeting tonight?

Me: Urm…Hi…Wasn't planning on it…you?

Tattoo Man: Thought I might give it miss like…no more said.

Me: Thanks…for the beer, thanks for the…

Tattoo Man: Adnams.

Paul McMahon – Dead Reckoning

Me: Adnams? Cheers.

Tattoo Man: Sláinte.

(both men raise glasses)

Tattoo Man: You're an early starter aren't you?

Me: An early riser? I am yeah, lots to do...catch the worm and all that.

Tattoo Man: Sitting here?

Me: Urm...yeah. For now yeah. You?

Tattoo Man: To speak the truth, I shall sit at this bar for as long as my faculties and gravity permits, and drink all my shrapnel.

Me: Sounds like a plan.

Tattoo Man: Barman, two brandies. You can get the next round in.

I do get the next round in, more out of obligation than of real willing, and we conduct our conversation from either end of the bar, not out of impoliteness but reluctance on my part to vacate my well-worn stool. Besides, there's no other person in the bar to mind our raised voices save the barman, and to them boring, loud conversations are an occupational hazard.

Paul McMahon – Dead Reckoning

Tattoo Man receives a phone call and takes it outside. I take the opportunity to enquire with the barman if the 'establishment' does tabs, as I am running out of change and I know the nearest cash point is over ten minutes away. He quite sensibly points out that I am not a regular and that he is not in the mood to get ripped off this lifetime, which I have to admire.

Windfall:

Tattoo Man comes back, full of the spice of life, and tells me he has just won £500 on a horse called 'Maiden Voyage' that his mate had put some money down on for him. He tells the barman he wants the finest champagne available to humanity and he wants it now. I feel like Marlow. The barman shrugs a sort of disinterested apology, offers him a cheap imitation 'Moet', and explains that his punters have no cause for celebration round here.

Two glasses are laid out on the bar and a bottle of nondescript fizzy stuff is cracked open. I'm grateful we're the only customers here as this ostentatious celebration is wholly incongruous to both the décor of this dingy pub and our individual attires, with me looking accurately like I slept in mine and Tattoo Man as if he stole his off a dead tramp. Plainly we must just look odd. Question: If there is no one around to witness, do you still *look* like a twat?

Drinks poured, Tattoo Man raises a glass to Maiden Voyage and we both neck our respective glasses in one. Tattoo Man pats his pockets down and swears, saying that he has left his phone somewhere in the bogs. He walks off out of the bar toward the toilets and comes back a short time later. He tells me he's lost it

Paul McMahon – Dead Reckoning

and asks if I can call it for him so he can hear it. I agree and he scrawls the number down on a beer mat much to the dissatisfaction of the barman.

Tattoo Man makes his way back toward the toilets as I dial the number.

The phone rings four times and I wait for the answer phone to kick in before trying again. Halfway through the fifth ring the phone is answered, and I hear a familiar voice-

Familiar voice: Got ya...

<u>Walk the plank</u>:

I drift toward the toilets, spaced-out with the phone pressed to my ear unable to speak, and push open the door looking for Tattoo Man. The smell of the urinals isn't what makes me sick, or the open window, or the realisation that I have to pick up the bar tab. What makes me sick this very instant is the familiar cockney voice at the end of the phone when he proudly introduces himself, formerly, as Tigger.

Tigger explains that he now has evidence stored on his SIM card - which will soon be jammed so far up his arse that you couldn't get it out with a veterinary glove - of my mobile phone making an incoming call to his mobile phone which, he reminds me, is an illegal article in one of her Majesty's Prisons. He explains that he simply wants me to do him a small one-off favour, and in

Paul McMahon – Dead Reckoning

return he will not reveal that a previously unblemished officer has been calling him in prison on an illicit mobile phone.

As if anticipating my first line of defence, he explains that he has fabricated a full story about how I have been trafficking items into him over the past few months. He has prepared a full backstory, with paid-up junkie witnesses, about how the arrangements started, and how we were connected by a tattooed outside associate who would be only too happy to confirm his claims to the Police for another bookies fee of £500.

I consider telling Tigger that I was on my way into work to murder him and make it look like suicide, which I am 99% sure is within my capabilities.

I consider telling Tigger to try his luck, that my renowned professionalism and good character would triumph in the end, but this bluff would cost me dearly.

In the end, after a long pause,

I simply agree to bring him a parcel.

Paul McMahon – Dead Reckoning

Periscope up:

I'm finding it hard to concentrate where they have deployed me for my short early shift this morning. My neck is aching from sleeping in a sitting position on the night bus all last night. My back is hurting from misjudging the volcanic showers in the staff locker room first thing this morning. I have a lot on my mind. My homelessness is right up there at the top of the list, right below my impending role as a drug trafficker into work. I have a little voice in my head that just won't shut up. I can't think straight and this voice is driving me up the wall, so I snap and take my radio earpiece out. This doesn't go down well with the Visits S/O, who is immediately dispatched by the Camera OSG to come and order me to put it back in, which I do begrudgingly. Apparently it is imperative that the floor patrol officers in the Visits Room are in constant audio contact with the camera room, mainly so that the Camera Room OSG can feel in a position of power I expect, but officially so that they can let the floor patrol officers know when they observe some 'little Herbert' trying to pass drugs to one of our prisoners. I can see the sense in this. I actually think that it's a great idea. In all the years that I have worked here I have never been deployed as floor patrol. It's a bit of a sprog job really. On the rare occasion I get jobbed down here from my Wing I usually get one of the plumb jobs sat on my arse ticking names off on the table allocation desk, or the Bingo board as it is known. But not today; the officers I am working with today have enough years between them to stretch back into the prehistoric age, so I'm lumbered with floor patrol and will just have to suck it up, and that's that.

'Visits' is widely acknowledged as being one of the most boring jobs in the prison. Nothing ever happens. More accurately, nothing is ever seen to happen. That is because the prison is usually so short-staffed that there is never a bloody Camera Room OSG anyway, and when there is they are usually a decrepit old codger

Paul McMahon – Dead Reckoning

anyway. Not today. Today I am being spoken to by 'Q'. His real name is something Greek and unpronounceable, but it starts with Q. The nickname however really works as he doesn't get the 'Bond reference', which everybody else does. Q loves the technology up there, the earpieces especially, and will give a constant running commentary on the position of 'individuals' hands and the changes in location of outer garments, should anybody be interested, throughout the course of the visiting session.

Q tells me it is 15:58hrs, meaning that there is two minutes left of visiting time. I do as instructed by Q, and walk down the aisles tapping prisoners on shoulders and telling them to finish their visits. As I approach the end of Row C, I stop in my tracks, as I see a face, neck and body I know. She is looking around nervously and laughing in the way that people do when they are trying to look ultra-cool, uber-relaxed.

Periscope down:

I cut through from Row C to Row D and turn back in the other direction moving away from her, tapping prisoner's shoulders but forgetting to actually tell them anything. Just then Q announces to all foot patrols over the radio net that he has identified a possible target. Thank fuck for that; this will hopefully pull me off in the other direction and give me somewhere to be, something to be engaged in for the final few minutes of the session. I cross my fingers in my pocket. The target is C8. The target is her. I carry on walking in the other direction, hoping that Q will see I am out of radius, but he doesn't. As if in retaliation for my earlier insubordination he announces my call sign and asks me to approach the target, C8. I hold my breath. There are so many reasons why I am scared about approaching her that I don't know which one to panic about first: if she pins the police visit on me I'm done for; if she acts like we are old friends in front of my colleagues, I am done for; if I have to jump on her and the whole ugly truth comes, out I am done for. In short, I am done for. Q is banging on in my ear, getting more and more irate. I flick a glance over to where the Visits S/O is standing listening to the radio exchange and he nods at me to do as I am told. I spin round incredibly slowly, wishing that she won't pass, hoping that she is just scratching an incredibly itchy fanny and that she is going to get up and say her goodbyes before I reach her, before she recognises me. Q is getting excited now, he is telling me that the hand is in her waist band and that she has taken something out. Q tells me that she has put something in her mouth, and is moving closer across the table. Q is now shouting so loud, he probably doesn't need the radio airwaves to engage, engage, ENGAGE!

There is nothing else for it; I have to be seen to do something. My job is on the line here, and I have to make a move. So I do make a move. Seated in D8, to my left, is sat an elderly women visiting Robinson. She is in a nun's habit, and has her arm in a sling. I run toward her quickly, to stop my brain intervening, and rugby tackle her off her chair, cupping her throat in my left hand on the way down to the floor to stop her swallowing - not that she has any gear in her mouth. I land on top of her, to gasps from the visiting hall and justifiable screams of objection from Robinson. In all the kerfuffle I can hear Q calling me a "fucking idiot", and screaming-

Q: C, C, C, C, C, C, C, C8, C8!

From underneath a now livid Robinson, and another couple of white shirts who have simply followed my lead, I can see my hooker friend French kissing her 'boyfriend'. Such a

Paul McMahon – Dead Reckoning

concentrated display of affection looks doubly incongruous when everybody else in the hall is up on their feet, shouting and waving their arms in the air. Whilst I am being pounded by Robinson, I can see my hooker friend saunter off toward the exit, swinging that arse of hers.

Visits are terminated, and once the visitors are vacated and the prisoners disbursed back the Wings, we get a chance to investigate what went wrong in the debrief. Q blames me, as it is my fault. I blame Q's Greek accent and diction, as it is an easy approach to take. Both the other white shirts fall in line and back me up, because I am an officer and Q is an OSG. Nothing like a bit of misplaced solidarity.

Between the Devil and the deep blue sea:

It has been a long morning. I enter 'The Compass' and acknowledge the landlord, who waits for me to walk the entire length of the saloon, settle myself into a stool and assemble my shrapnel on the bar before telling me, in an insufferably slow fashion, that I am baaaaarred. Apparently patrons who walk out without paying disproportionately high prices for Eastern European champers are not welcome in his little hovel. I apologise profusely and offer to settle the bill immediately, which he accepts equally instantaneously. I'm considering, in the spirit of new beginnings, telling him to keep the change, but there is evidently no change forthcoming.

I ask for a pint and the landlord pours me an Adnams, leaving it his side of no man's land, across the beer mats in what is clearly now enemy territory. In what I consider a wholly unnecessary gesture, he whips out my reserve blue beer token, on top of which were stacked a number of pint-price change sculptures, and lurches off to the till. This time he returns with my change, slamming it down in front of me. I glance down to inspect his integrity and count a two pound coin, fifty-pence piece, and an extremely small, tightly coiled, spring.

Actual conversation No.12:

Me: I think this must have got mixed up in the 20p's.

Landlord: Nope.

Me: Well, it's coming back over the bar next drink. This currency is no good elsewhere.

Landlord: It's yours.

Me: Er…right. What am I supposed to do with it?

Landlord: Shove it up your arse.

Me: What?

Landlord: That's what he said. He just told me you would know what he meant. Fucking space cases the pair of ya'.

Me: Who?

Landlord: Paddy. He gave me a score and told me to give that to you if you tried to come back in here, which I said you wouldn't, but you have; so drink your pint, take your spring and fuck off.

Paul McMahon – Dead Reckoning

I have not slept in days with anxiety, suffering nights of perpetual torment over what weight, of which drug, Tigger was to force me to mule in past my colleagues. All for this. Piss taking cunt.

I get it. I think I get it. I don't get it. What a Prick.

Where ever I lay my hat is my home:

Homeless Melvin is just as hospitable as he was last night it seems, judging from the empty bottle of Bollinger sat beside my boots at the end of this double bed I don't recognise. He has woken me on time for work, as he apparently promised that he would, with a coffee and a slice of toast. Wholemeal. He thanks me again for taking all this so sportingly, considering all the pound coins I have drunkenly tossed him over the years. He is still astonished, quite-frankly, that I reacted so calmly after spotting him on the night bus last night, chatting into his iPhone donning his polished, brown leather winkle pickers on his way back from snorting lines of ketamine at Stringfellows. Melvin is right; normally I would find this sort of thing utterly reprehensible, and deserving of an almighty kicking but I have bigger things on my mind, and don't feel comfortable lecturing him about morality when I am more than likely going to be using my arse, from this point in, for an unethical function that it was most certainly not designed for. So I tell him it's fine. He tells me, by way of explanation, that if he ceased the practice of begging, he would have to claim the dole, which is a very reasonable argument - almost admirable I tell him. He says he is doing so well out of begging that only a fool would stop, that his specific London spot yields so much financially he would be a mug to pass it up. He proudly announces to me that he

Paul McMahon – Dead Reckoning

is an expert in 'spot' selection, and discloses to me something about an algorithm for pedestrian footfall and the average hourly donation of a tourist, but I am so overwhelmed I can't take it all in.

The 'House of Correction':

I am overwhelmed with feelings of relief. Relief, the way I see it, that Melvin's predicament presents me with the prospect of guaranteed 'residency' - out of pure guilt, if nothing else, as a way to sincerely atone for the lie he 'hath perpetrated upon me'; that's my angle. My back is in shipshape fashion after a night on his spare mattress, which is eminently more comfortable than a bus seat, and I make this known to him without labouring the point too much. Melvin is a man of good manners and, after a little pause, he tells me that I'm welcome to bed down again tonight if I need to. I do.

D-Day:

I leave Melvin's with a key, which I add to my own bunch. Almost all the keys on this bunch are superfluous to my life in its current state and serve absolutely no purpose, but I can't bear to part with them; there are many memories in this bunch. I find their weight comforting in my pocket, and they make a superb improvised knuckle duster, should the need so occur. The spring I also spontaneously attach to my bunch in a moment of inspiration. It is not going up my arse if I can help it. I inspect the bunch and am satisfied it appears as if it belongs, metal amongst metal alongside its keyed brethren. I'm so confident I don't even remember that it has joined the jingling and jangling as I breech PSO 1215, and traffic it through the gate lodge.

Paul McMahon – Dead Reckoning

Nobody knows were the shoe pinches 'cept the wearer:

I immediately feel ashamed of myself for judging Gav. This must have been how he felt the first time he betrayed us all. The briefing is well underway and the S/O offers the floor to each of us sitting round the circle, in case any of us want to add anything that has been missed, to enlighten any of the rest of the team to anything we have heard that might compromise our security today. The domino of "No Sir" curves round to me and I desperately want to open up - I want to open up like those alcoholic hippies did at the meeting - but I don't.

Passing the Rubicon:

When I look through the observation glass of his cell door, Tigger is lying in his shithole, decadently smoking a roll up and blowing lopsided smoke rings into the air. Uncharacteristically, I *almost* knock on the cell door, realising at the last nanosecond and so modifying my move, morphing it seamlessly into a weird door-lunging motion. My entrance is preposterous.

Tigger doesn't move. If pets were allowed he would have had procured himself a white Persian pussy, just to be able to stroke it villainously in this very moment. Tigger's finger gestures me to sit down. I don't want to sit down; I want to stub his cigarette out into his eyeball and stamp on his throat. I sit down. Tigger tells me to turn my radio off so we can talk. I don't want to turn my radio off; I want to press my personal alarm and then head-butt the wall, stitch-up style. I turn the radio off.

Paul McMahon – Dead Reckoning

Actual conversation No.13:

Tigger: So you got the thing.

Me: The spring thing. Yeah I got it.

Tigger: Let me see it.

Me: Fuck you, give me the mobile.

Tigger: Look you corrupt cunt, let's not pretend that you've any room for manoeuvre here. Get what I'm saying, sweetcheeks? Give me the fucking spring.

Me: Why a poxy spring?

Tigger: Testing compliance. I thought about asking you to wear in a set of suspenders under your uniform for a laugh. To heighten your sense of humiliation, see? But I didn't want you get the wrong idea.

I unhook the little coiled spring from my house keys and throw it at Tigger far too hard. It bounces off his forehead and he scrambles on the floor of the cell frantically after it. Stop. Tigger stands triumphantly, holding his badge of victory, and smiles a toothlessly offensive smile. It starts to dawn on me all too late, just as Tigger reaches down behind his back end where his tail ought to be, that this insignificant little coil might be significant after all. Monumentally significant, in fact, being that Tigger's new facial expression perfectly personifies the sensation of plugging an alien object up one's sphincter.

Paul McMahon – Dead Reckoning

There ensues a stop in time in which I am calculating the odds of being able to extract a spring from an uncooperatively clenched arse, what level of noise would emanate from an individual having this procedure performed on them, if this would be overheard, and if anybody would actually respond - or even care.

Spring in his step:

As it turns out this is no ordinary spring. Tigger evidently feels so confident in his sphincter-safe's impenetrability that he goes onto enlighten me about this hitherto extraneous object. He reveals that it is, in fact, a *unique* spring, designed to act in synchronicity alongside the multitude of other tiny, metallic components that had been smuggled into the establishment, piece by piece, inside Gav's rectum; parts which, when assembled, are known collectively amongst those in the know as a 'Pocket Glock' (Model 26) 9mm.

I would like to kill Tigger with his trigger.

The penny drops:

I am totally fucked. There is no explaining my way out of this one. In the true spirit of the criminal justice system, the facts in this case are totally surpassed by Tigger's indisputable concoction of untruths. Bravo. All that remains to be disclosed is the end game. So I ask. Then I wish I hadn't.

Paul McMahon – Dead Reckoning

Leonine contract:

My role in Tigger's self-titled 'grand masterplan' is to act as a mule for him now that Gav has met his 'demise'. He has managed to replace Gav on a temporary basis with a multi-tasking hooker who knows half of the prison population; however, this isn't preferable, as in the long run, drug-muling through visits is too risky. Because of this, Tigger decrees that I shall attend my last shift of each month with a shipment of gear up my back passage, which he requires I then pass onto him during the course of the morning. This is all.

The day is fixed and Tigger makes me put a little asterisk in my shift diary, which he also marks on his cell calendar. He tells me that I will need to give him my address in order for him to arrange for the drugs to be delivered to me the night before. I take immediate evasive action, and tell Tigger that I'm between addresses at the moment that we will have to use somewhere temporary this month. Tigger does not look pleased about this, apparently my little act of trickery displeases him, but he asks me to suggest somewhere. I tell him that I have access to Gav's address, and suggest that if he has been arranging delivery there then it seems convenient to use it for one more drop whilst I arrange for a permanent roof over my head. After a moment to ponder this, Tigger says that for this month alone he will allow the drop to be done there. He makes it very clear to me, however, that he *will* need to know where I live and how very easy it is to get my address off the electoral roll or from the council, without having to ask one of his associates to follow me home after a shift. He insists on being made aware of my address as soon as I have sorted one. Then I really will be in his pocket.

Before I leave I ask Tigger why he has chosen me. Tigger smiles, looking pleased I have asked him this question.

Paul McMahon – Dead Reckoning

Actual conversation No.14:

Tigger: Because you are perfect.

Me: How so?

Tigger: Let me explain. My 'link man' has to be below radar, completely above suspicion. I've watched you. I've watched you, watching us. You hate me, you hate *us* - all of us - and everybody *knows* you hate us. All the cons know you hate us, the other screws know you hate us, the Governor, the security department, the Doctors, the IMB - *everybody* knows *you* hate *us*. So the idea, the very notion that *you* would do *anything* that would benefit any *one* of us is unimaginable. So you Mr B, *you* are perfect.

I have to hand it to him. He really isn't quite the retarded doughnut that he comes across as. There is a sort of genius logic about the whole idea. It is true that I am the last person that would ever do this, or be suspected of doing this, so why am I doing it? I'm doing it because, despite being desperate to, I can't come up with a single idea to get myself out of this fucking mess.

Tigger has become an important player in the prison economy. His reputation as a reliable supplier has been established due to his dependable pre-death accomplice/logistics manager, Gav, and subsequently, if only on a temporary basis, his stand in cover, Jackie. Demand has increased, as has supply and in turn profit, the spoils of which adorn the cell - Pioneer separates and brand new Nike Air size 8s.

Paul McMahon – Dead Reckoning

I have had a bad day. Actually I have had a terrible day. The sort of day that makes you want to jump off an extremely tall building. I am not, however, going to jump off an extremely tall building. Someone has to clean all that up, and suicide is a bit of an intellectual cop out. So I am going to get absolutely smashed - on Melvin's guilt. You have got to milk the udder while the cow is full. I reach Melvin's very real residential address with unexpected speed. I haven't really prepared myself for the session I am about to embark on, as I have been worrying about my liberty, reputation, and general safety. As I walk into the front room I find Melvin hunched over a wrap of some sort of powder or another on the coffee table. He spins round with a £50 pound note up his nose and greets me with wide open arms, and a wild look in his eye. He is holding a bottle of wine in one hand, and offers it to me after he has released me from this surprisingly awkward one-sided hug. I commandeer Melvin's bottle of wine while he is crawling around the carpet looking for the lighter that he is holding in his other hand. By the time he has realised that he is holding it, I have downed the remainder of the bottle and am searching through his cabinets looking for some whiskey. It's a whiskey sort of a day. Melvin is talking really quickly about shopping while he is cutting up a line with an American Express card. The wine is kicking in, and I take a second to brace myself for getting totally shitfaced.

The Nth degree:

Melvin is now freaking me out. I don't think he is doing it on purpose but he is freaking the fuck out of me with logic of a different order. I like logic, fuck knows I love the stuff, but whatever Melvin has given me to snort has blown my brain. Melvin apparently wants to take me into logic orbit and I don't want to go. Melvin announces that he is going to show me just how 'exciting' maths is, as he scrawls out a long set of Algebra on the fridge with a felt tip pen, whilst jabbering on about how malleable the laws of Maths are if you are genius.

$$(n+1)^2 - (2n+1) = n^2$$
$$(n+1)^2 - (2n+1) - \quad (2n+1)$$

$$= n^2 - n(2n+1)$$
$$(n+1)^2 - (n+1)(2n+1) =$$

$$n^2 - n(2n+1)$$
$$(n+1)2-$$
$$(n+1)(2n+1)+(2n+1)^2/4 =$$

$$n^2-n(2n+1)+(2n+1)^2/4$$
$$[(n+1)-(2n+1)/2]^2 = [n-(2n+1)/2]^2$$
$$(n+1) - (2n+1)/2 = n - (2n+1)/2$$
$$N+1 = n$$
$$1 = 0$$

Now I don't know if Melvin *is* a genius, but I am 100% sure he *is* a fucking nutcase, and no, this is *not* exciting; it's fucking terrifying. I mean how the holy fuck can 1 = 0. How the fuck am I supposed to be sure I won't just suddenly fall off the ground if "1" decides that it doesn't fancy being itself anymore. Well I'm not having it. "1" is *not* a transsexual. It's a fucking red-blooded son of a bitch with a big phallic body. What the fuck is Melvin going on about; why is he still talking?!

Paul McMahon – Dead Reckoning

Actual conversation No?

Me: SHUT UP YOU MAD CUNT! I'm having a fucking whitey here, you lunatic!

Melvin: Breath through it man, this is my world.

Me: I don't want to be in your world, you fucking maniac. We only came into the Galley to get some more wine, and you go and fuck with the cosmos.

Melvin: Sorry, but....

Me: Don't be sorry! Just rub it off, I don't want to look at it, make it go away!

Melvin: That's the world, man

Me: That's not the fucking world, you mad bastard, just leave it alone, and give me the FUCKING GROG!

Melvin does give me the wine, but he doesn't wipe the fridge, which means I have to get the fuck out the Galley before I explode with paranoia. I can feel oblivion creeping up on me as I am absolutely wasted. I think I better get some more booze down me to speed up my collapse, as I really don't want to end up down the Police Station again and lose my job. Think about something else.

My head is extremely painful. I have a little shuffle around to check if I have any injuries before I try and move. Luckily I don't. I have a quick look around to see if I am in Melvin's spare room, on his spare bed, which I think I am. All in all, this is a pretty

Paul McMahon – Dead Reckoning

good start to the day. I don't have to be at work, so I look at my watch hoping most of the day has gone as I don't have anywhere to be or anything to do. Luckily I'm well into the afternoon, so I don't have to wait too much longer before my very existence has a clear purpose again. There is nothing to do except contemplate my quandary. As my S/O always says, "Prior Planning Prevents Piss Poor Performance".

A good lather is half the shave:

I have only come up with a plan! A plan so cunning, that I am actually looking forward to seeing if it will work. I am aware that in a Category B local there are not many staff searches, and the searches that are conducted are executed badly. I am generally aware of their scheduling, as are all the other staff who drink; loose lips sink ships, and there is nothing more talked about in the staff club over a few pints than that which is supposed to be restricted information -the sexy stuff, the secret squirrel stuff. However, let us just suppose that the security department were to manage to pull off an actual 'surprise' staff search. I need to have a manner of smuggling in the drugs which is both clandestine and undetectable. The clandestine bit I have already ticked off - the old arse suitcase has that sorted. The undetectable bit is the bit that has had me most concerned, until now. I have heard, having never worked down there, that visitors have tried to mask the smell of drugs from the drugs dogs, in a variety of ways. The most frequent method is wrapping the drugs in several layers of cling film, whilst wearing fresh latex gloves after each layer to avoid transferring the smell from each cling film layer to the next, and then smothering the package in perfume before nestling it up the front or back bottom. This sometimes works and sometimes doesn't, depending which side of the basket the dog got out of that particular morning. My stroke of genius is that I shall not attempt to mask the smell, I shall embrace it.

Today, while performing the daily Locks Bolts & Bars check, I tactically jump on the new occupant of B2-01 as he is reaching for his dressing gown. In hindsight I probably should have wound him up and made him bite, but the dressing gown could have easily have been a weapon. I wasn't to know. Think about something else. In the melee I managed not to rip my trousers, despite my best efforts. I have to hurriedly fashion the rip after my rescue party's arrival, while they are occupied administering a kicking upon the naked lad. It occurs to me post-rip that the dimensions of said rip are more important than I had initially given credence to. Too small a rip and I would attract suggestions of self-repair, too large a rip and I would attract ridicule en route off the Wing from other prisoners, who would interpret this as an sign of personal weakness and chink in the amour of our natural authority. This epiphany comes all too late, as the rip I have managed to craft exposes not only my eggshell/formerly white cotton boxer shorts, but extends down to my ankle. I am an inch or so from one legged clown flares. As the perpetrator is cuff-carried down to the segregation unit, Oscar 1 appears and shows genuine concern for the wellbeing of my uniform. He assures me that the prisoner will be disciplined for the assault perpetrated upon my trousers and ruffles my hair patronisingly over the spot where I have been punched, before sending me off home as I can't be expected to work after what has just happened to my trousers. Yes I'm fine thanks, Sir.

Today-Grow the seed:

This morning I wear in my last remaining pair of clean, crisp, new uniform trousers from the bottom of my locker, and spend the entire day strategically bemoaning the scratching and itching that is being perpetrated upon the inside of my thighs by my LAST and "ONLY PAIR OF TROUSERS". I manage to crowbar this itchy trouser moan into unrelated conversations about at what exact point bread becomes toast, and the effect that the wind chill factor has on the formation of ice. Amazingly enough, every member of uniform staff I complain in the presence of becomes irate in empathy as they tell of their own itchy trouser stories. By the end of the day, the Prison Officers Association have discussed the issue at local branch committee level, and have decided to formerly write to the National Executive Committee asking for action to be taken on both the substandard materials used to construct our poor uniform and the supply problems we are faced with in procuring replacements. Yes, you can cut our pay, and ignore the ever increasing levels of staff assaults upon the membership, but we will be exercising zero fucking tolerance over itchy thighs. Unity is strength comrades.

Today-Harvest the seed:

This morning I find a small quantity of gear during a cell search carried out on a random junkie, courtesy of a post-sale tip off from Tigger. It wasn't a pleasant transaction and Tigger wants it dealt with. I am more than happy to oblige, not only as it fits in with my plan, but it keeps him sweet. I record the particulars of this search on all the relevant paperwork - professionally for a change - so there is perfect audit trail, and seal the gear in an evidence bag which I store in my "…only pair of trousers" pocket, en route to the evidence locker in the Security Department. I stop along the way to uncharacteristically converse with every colleague whom I spot and share the success of my find, not to mention my itchy thighs.

It's lunch time and I'm reflecting on the level of professional admiration I've received this morning, partly as a result of my cell search find, but mostly due to my growing reputation as the Officer spearheading the uprising against the uniform infidels in HQ. It feels good. I have been so plagued by supporters all though the morning that I've chosen to eat my sandwich at the desk on the 1s landing, volunteering to do the lunch hour shift that should have been covered by Gav, according the detail - if he were alive - or 'Mr Green', if he had finished his initial training and started yet. I could have elected to go down to the club and partake in more discussions about our 'tactics' for the upcoming uniform rebellion that is currently occupying every staff get together, but it's all getting a bit out of hand really. There's not much to stimulate or distract me here from worrying about my predicament, apart from a pile of prisoner applications scattered across the desk which are in need of attention. I give them enough of my attention to facilitate their journey into the bin on the left of the desk. I sit staring at my sandwich that Melvin made me this morning, as I find simple food inspiring.

To cut the Gordian knot:

I shut down the main engine of my cognisance, in order to indulge my palate in its own little private voyage into a savoury-sweet stupor. In the background my brain is flipping and whirring until, in one near perfect stream of sub-consciousness ...

Sandwich Cheese and Tomato Tomatoes have skin Humans have skin Black skin White skin Pierced skin Tattooed skin Tattooed Man Alcoholic Alcohol Anchor & Hope Midday champagne lost phone Called phone Stitched up Lunch time Call phone. Call phone Bingo - Knot cut.

Paul McMahon – Dead Reckoning

The response time from Security is rather impressive considering that they are all a bunch of lazy cunts. It's Oily that puffs in unexpectedly, quickly and alone. Oily has just redeployed to the group today and allegedly has to show willingness. Strictly speaking, I'm not allowed to enter a cell at lunch time without Oscar 1 and at least three members of staff, after having first informed the control room; having said that, this policy was not written with Oily in mind. I brief Oily on the 'facts', namely that I have just stumbled across a note on the floor of the staff common room off the landing 'grassing' that there is a phone being used at lunch time somewhere on the Wing. Oily has brought with him a small PDA device that management brought last year, wanting motivated staff to use it for detecting mobile phone signals within the prison. I have heard about this little bit of kit before and know it to be accurate down to the precise cell. This particular device still has the protective plastic cover on the display panel and appears to have never been out of its box. Whilst Oily is attempting to unfold the instructions with his unfit-for-purpose fingers, I punch my pin number into the landline phone on the front desk to get an outside line. Oily creeps as much as his 20+ stone allows him, up to the 3s landing and turns on the PDA. At this point I dial Tigger's phone number. A ringing sound emanates from the receiver and a sense of excitement rushes over me. The next sound I hear is in slightly delayed stereo as an unfamiliar voice answers,

Voice: Hel…..oooooooshhiiiiit!

I don't know exactly what is happening upstairs, but I can hear the distant sound of what I think is a bolt springing on an opening cell door followed by a thud, which I assume is thick steel denting concrete wall as the door is flung open by an angry animal. Down the receiver I can hear a wet thud, which I very much hope is Tigger's head exploding upon impact with Oily's bowling ball fist. Then nothing. I put the receiver down and sprint up to the 3s landing. I rush up to Tigger's door and push it with my open hand, which stays where it is as I smash straight into the unyielding, and

Paul McMahon – Dead Reckoning

locked cell door. Through my watery gaze, like a toddler after an encounter with a patio door, I can see a body lying further down the landing. I got the wrong door. I don't understand. I make my way toward the shape and wipe my eyes with the hand that is not stemming the flow of blood from my flattened hooter. The newly unconscious con is a nobody. I look up, then up some more toward Oily who is holding a mobile phone to his ear. Nobody there he informs me. I ask Oily if I can have a look and Oily says yes, handing me the phone. Immediately I access the incoming calls log and, lo and behold, scroll down to see my mobile phone number in all its 11 digit glory staring back at me. This is the self-same number that the prison has on record for calling me out in an emergency, like a hostage scene. What happens now is unplanned, poorly thought through, and utterly unsatisfactory. I obviously can't slip from here, as the toilet I want to drop the phone in is too far away and round the corner in the actual cell. I walk in to the cell, telling Oily that I want to open it up to check if there is a SIM card inside, and flip the back off the battery as I go. In one slinky movement, I 'slip' on nothing and melodramatically drop the phone down the loo, before clattering to the ground accidentally on purpose. As a late addition I let out my sound effect after the manoeuvre, which just makes me look plain stupid. It couldn't have gone worse if I'd tried.

Oily looks confused. My little cabaret doesn't appear to have fooled him in the slightest. It is now time for some monumental blagging action, the like of which has never been seen before.

A lie hath no feet; it cannot stand alone:

I tell Oily a tale of intrigue and of cunning, of double lives and covert human intelligence sources. My improvisation skills are a surprise to myself, and I find that I am delivering a convincing

Paul McMahon – Dead Reckoning

pitch. The boiled down facts of my subterfuge are that this phone has been stolen off another prisoner, the identity of which I do not know, who was being used as a 'super grass'. This particular phone had been issued to him by a certain Governor on behalf of the Old Bill as the intelligence is of such operational significance a risk assessment deemed it proportionate to allow this prisoner to be in possession of such an unauthorised article, to enable direct communication to his Metropolitan police handler. Oily interrupts and asks questions. Lots of questions. So many questions that I can't remember exactly what I've said in the first place and don't know whether these lies fit. I'm really nervous now. I tell Oily, in response to his latest query, that the phone was stolen off this 'super grass' prisoner by a gang of 'Yardies' who had been after his old school JVC boom-box; in which he had hidden it; unfortunately the handset had been secreted in the front housing of the tape deck when it was nicked. I congratulate Oily on his find, as clearly this unconscious shape on the landing floor was the little bastard that had lifted it. I round off my monologue with an obligatory "I have said too much". In my head there is applause, and the front row are leading my standing ovation whilst throwing flowers onto the stage at my feet.

If it looks like a Duck & quack's like a Duck:

Oily tells me, expressionless, that he is disappointed in me. Bollocks. This could go either way. He tells me that whatever shit has gone down that I should be able to trust him enough to level with him. I want to level with him. Why didn't I just level with him? He looks angry, and as if to illustrate this point he punches the unconscious prisoner in the arse who, as if to illustrate his unconsciousness, doesn't react. Oily tells me that he wants to trust me. After a pause, he announces that in light of the fact I have let him in on the most exciting thing ever to happen to him, he'll overlook my initial dishonesty and theatrics, now that I have laid it

Paul McMahon – Dead Reckoning

all bare. I'm getting 'a touch' he makes clear, just this once mind. I remind Oily that he can't mention this operation to anybody, as it would compromise an enormous investigation, and he agrees to keep his gob well and truly shut provided that he be my wing man on any future 'missions' that I may be sent. That, and I never lie to him again. Deal.

The phone is retrieved from the loo, bagged and tagged, and HCC are called for the prisoner who has snoozed through the details of his parallel existence.

We unlock at 14:00 on the dot. By 14:01hrs Tigger is at the door Oily had smashed in not half an hour previous. Jackpot.

Bad Heroin:

Upon reporting for duty in the gate lodge, I'm told that there's a lockdown on my Wing today. In the briefing we are told that the Mandatory Drug Testing figures are through the roof with positive results and the Security Department believes there is a vast amount of drugs in the prison. Genius deduction. What has finally tipped the balance into actually doing something about it has been the Area Manager breathing down the neck of the Number One Governor this morning, due to a prisoner overdosing last night. Upon doing the early roll count this morning one had been found dead. "Slumped over in a pool of his own vomit," I am told by Doreen, who I'm sitting next to. She is munching her way through a packet of peanuts, listening to the briefing being delivered by 'Welshy', the dedicated search team S/O. Welshy is wearing his earpiece, which he reserves for special operations so prisoners cannot hear any radio traffic. He is dressed in an embroidered uniform polo shirt, which he has personally had adorned with his name, rank and number, and wearing his self-purchased non-prison issue webbing, and tactical belt, to which he has attached various pouches of all shapes and sizes and in which he transports vital DST equipment such as a mini Maglite, spare search gloves, and confectioneries. Welshy has his shiny, black combat trousers tucked into, and puffed out from, the ankles of his Magnum boots, the toes of which he has polished to within an inch of their leather lives.

A lot of thought has evidently been invested by Welshy into *how* to present this briefing; less thought into any actual content. There is a single slide up on the projector screen which looks like a photo of some powder; some nondescript powder, of a nondescript colour, in some nondescript cellophane. Such insight. Welshy refers to this slide behind him continually whilst addressing the hall, as if in an attempt to hypnotically distract us from the fact that he is talking a complete load of bollocks. Welshy triumphantly unveils his plan that we will be searching every prisoner on the wing and that intelligence suggests we would be looking for…drugs. Mastermind.

Welshy reassures the hall that the dedicated search team - or the DST as he insists on referring to them in their acronymic splendour - will be *supporting* the searching pairs of wing officers from a position within a side office, prepared to book any evidence that may be found during this operation. So essentially not doing any searching whatsoever, dedicated or otherwise. Sheer tactical genius.

I am paired up with, and on the insistence of, Oily, who I have been trying to avoid. We join a queue of staff waiting to be issued with a search sheet which corresponds to a specific cell and its occupants to be searched. As we get nearer the front of the cue Oily winks at me. I pretend not to have seen it. I allow a second or so to pass and then glance back at him hoping to catch the facial expression of a man who realises what a monumental prick he is being, when he winks at me again. No ordinary wink this time around but a pantomime wink. If he wasn't in possession of enough dirt on me to get me fired ten times over, or so ridiculously hard, I would kick him square in the gonads this very second, so help me Buddha. This is not going to work. What a huge lumbering liability.

As we get to the front of the queue, Welshy looks up with a blank search sheet and spots Oily. He smiles and pulls over an alphabetical list of all the prisoners on the wing. He twiddles his finder which he holds over the list, then plunges it down upon the sheet saying "yup". Luckily we are not given Tigger. Unluckily we are given French.

French stinks. He stands at 6' 4" and weighs in at approximately 19st meaning there is a lot of him to odourise the atmosphere. French is a conundrum. French is actually English. He hates the French almost as much as he hates Blacks, Jews and Women, attitudes he advertises on his skin; he is covered in offense from head to foot. The most observable example to those who don't have the pleasure of strip searching him, is a barcode across the back of his neck which bears the numbers 14, 88, 100%, paying homage to David Lane, Heil Hitler, and pure Aryan respectively. French is *also* a Muslim! You would be forgiven for thinking otherwise owing to the fact that has a Cross etched into his back, a swastika on either forearm, and the butt of a pistol carved into his stomach just above his waistline. The state of his cell, specifically of his religious artefacts, similarly makes his faith difficult to believe as French has his 'Holy' Quran on the floor in the corner of his cell, under a irreverent pair of soiled boxers, and his prayer mat folded up into a cushion on top of his filthy toilet seat. It's a sight I would love the blinkered Imam to see, not to mention the pictures of naked grannies cut out of his monthly periodical '50+' which are

Paul McMahon – Dead Reckoning

plastered to the wall over his bed with toothpaste (?). There is also some sort of noise coming out of the stereo, within which I can make out the occasional 'Nigger' and 'Fuck', all of which I don't believe are strictly in keeping with the principles of Islam. Nonetheless, French is registered Muslim and needs to be searched prior to Jumna as it is Friday, and not even the presence of deadly Class A narcotics and a fatality can disrupt this most important of events, according to the Governor.

I ask French if he would like to be present during the searching of his legal paperwork. He declines, but insists that a drugs dog not be allowed to enter his cell as it would render his property defiled upon contact with its saliva in the eyes of Allah. French completes this sentence without even a hint of satire. I tell French that if we used a dog we would offer him a complete change of bed linen and deliver a complimentary bottle of house champagne should this occur, and offer him my sincerest assurance that all his religious artefacts will be treated with the utmost respect. Serve returned. 15 - all.

One of the DST staff collects French from outside the cell and helpfully escorts him to the holding room for us. I push the door to, and turn to find Oily has begun the search, thumbing through a box of Jizz magazines at the foot of the bed. The cell is small enough with Oily in it without the White Elephant making the situation even more uncomfortable for me.

I pick up a sealed pot of E45 Cream which has a few tell-tale scuffs around the seal. While investigating I flick the kettle on and then inspect the tub in my hand. The small travel kettle bubbles up and I pour the water into the sink before tossing the tub into a steaming hot bath. Oily is still thumbing through the porn. To be fair there is a lot of it. It looks like it's sorted into categories of some sort, as there are makeshift tabs that look like

Paul McMahon – Dead Reckoning

they have been ripped out of an address book at intervals poking out of the pile. Clever. I pluck the pot of E45 out of the sink. The pot is now hot to the touch and supple, as it has expanded in the heat. With a little pressure on the sides of the pot, and using a plastic knife as a jemmy, the lid and seal pop off with ease.

The surface of the cream is disturbed. Dead give-away. Normally it should look like a close-up HD freeze-frame of a vanilla yogurt a millisecond after its surface had been penetrated by a plummeting pea. It should have a factory-fashioned cone-like wave protruding from its surface like a nipple. It doesn't. It looks like the top of a homemade shepherd's pie with the criss-cross of a dragged fork. I spin the knife round in my hand and plunge it down into the cream. It stops short of what should be the bottom.

I prise the knife-stopping object up through the gunge and pluck it out with my gloved hand. It is unclear what it is, so I throw it into the sink. The surrounding cream falls off, unveiling a small, orange, oval plastic container, which looks very much like the innards of a Kinder egg. Upon investigation - and the eventual opening - it transpires that it looks like a Kinder egg for that's what it is; however, instead of an annoyingly flimsy toy, within it appears to be a rather large amount what I suspect to be heroin. Tigger's heroin.

Oily is still thumbing the porn. He appears to be engrossed in a teen magazine featuring a flat-chested childlike centrefold that he is eye-fucking. Oily seems oblivious to my find and an idea dawns on me, one so thrilling that it sends goose pimples down my arms and causes my scrotum to contract. I squish the Kinder egg back into the goop and shepherd's pie the top, before pushing it all back together and continuing on through the toiletries, just in time for Oily to announce that he has found something in between the pages of *Amateur Babes* - Oily has uncovered a shiv. This

Paul McMahon – Dead Reckoning

improvised weapon has evidently been made with some craftsmanship. The body of the weapon is constructed out of a prison issue toothbrush, around the base of which is wrapped a length of ripped bed sheet which appears to act as a grip for the handle. The business end of the weapon has three razor blades melted-in along its length, running parallel to each other at their base and fanning out slightly at their blade edge. A clever design as the victim is cut thrice making the stitching process impossible; leaving them 'striped' with an ugly, and rather large, scar. Oily is very happy with himself and slides the 'tool' into an evidence tube.

Traffic:

Today I plug the small Kinder egg up my Gary Glitter. The process is not as unpleasant as I had imagined initially. I have given much thought to the 'insemination' and have decided, in my view rather cleverly, to coat the outside of the egg in lubricant. Not having any *actual* lubricant I opted for some olive oil. Extra Virgin. This enables me to slide the egg up my back passage without any need for coercion. Now it is up there, however, it feels a little greasy, and I hope very much it doesn't lead me to involuntarily drop the golden egg out when it's inappropriate to do so. I catch the bus in from Melvin's even though it is literally round the corner, as I don't want to disturb the cargo too much. This is it. This is what I have been building up to with my uniform rebellion and my itchy trouser bullshit all week. I tentatively walk into the Gate lodge, telling myself that there is absolutely nothing to worry about. I reassure myself that I can afford to be all snug and cosy in the knowledge that, even if a search dog sniffs my arse and decides to indicate on me, I have the perfect cover story that any officer that has come within a mile of me this week will be able to validate. Predictably enough, after all the planning and preparation I have put in over the last week, there isn't a sniffer dog or a search, not even anyone in the Gate lodge giving keys out. I am buzzed in

Paul McMahon – Dead Reckoning

through gate P10 to get my own keys. Incredible. This anti-climax has a detrimental impact upon my mood, and I arrive on the wing late morning, mourning my opportunity to feel clever and laud it over my clueless colleagues.

Reconnaissance Ob's:

French bumps into several scumbags during the morning domestic period that immediately follows unlock. The Kinder egg I found in his cell is definitely heroin, yes, but I have been sweating and itching with paranoia ever since arriving on the wing, wondering if it is actually Tigger's stash after all. Is it, in fact, just possible that French is operating on his own? I wonder if he has the 'minerals' to be in direct competition with Tigger. So I watch. When you know what to look for, it's all so obvious. Tigger is sitting on the landing a little way down from me, innocuously smoking a cigarette and 'reading' a copy of *Club International*, directly opposite where French is leaning outside his cell. French is being very 'sociable', under what looks like the watchful eye of Tigger. He pats a few backs, has his patted by many, shakes a few hands and has his high-fived by a disproportionately high number of scumbags. Amongst all of this I spot the palm off to Harris the 'superjunkie' clear as day. The pass is made a heartbeat after French flashes a look at Tigger, and Tigger flashes a subtle nod at French in return. Superjunkie now heads straight for the shower, where I imagine he is about to magic away the parcel in the habituated manner responsible for the onset of so many a prolapsed prison rectum. The gear should be safe up his rusty sheriff's badge until lunchtime, whereupon I imagine he will evacuate the blockage in order to cook it up and get super-high. I know exactly how he feels. Sure as eggs is eggs, he exits the shower in what would have been Guinness record-breaking shower time, in the same stinking state and clothing in which he entered, and heads for his cell. Bingo.

Paul McMahon – Dead Reckoning

As this place is such a shithole to work in, I'm able to cash in on the fact the turnover of staff is so rapid nobody knows anybody else's name. I phone through to the front desk in my best random Scots accent, adding French's name to the afternoon doctor's list without so much as a 'who the fuck are you?" With French absent this afternoon, I reckon I'll be able to get in there and swap the Kinder egg containers, so one has a real surprise in it.

At afternoon unlock French is called down to the 1s for the Doctor. He doesn't refuse as only a fool would turn down the opportunity to do a bit of grafting - you never look a gift-dealer in the mouth. This surprise appointment is a prime opportunity to badger the doctor about increasing the dosage of whatever painkiller he has talked his way into being prescribed for some phantom back injury or another. Once cheeked, these are fantastic currency with which to buy burn or smack, or pay a junkie to 'Pot' a screw.

Oh shit:

The smell is so potent that I momentarily forget myself, opening my mouth to scream, meaning it drips down my top lip into my mouth. I begin to retch at the taste and am so distracted by spasms that I forget to *not* open my eyes, which immediately start stinging with the salty urea. Just to top things off, my misery is compounded when my head is compounded.....

Deleted memory code execution 49555

Paul McMahon – Dead Reckoning

I don't know why I am laying on the floor. Somebody is shouting about a contract, and something about fucking someone's wife. Everything is in black and white. I could be in *Raging Bull*.

I become aware of faces standing over me all speaking at once. They are all out of focus and the sound is dull, like I'm watching a film underwater. There is one a little more in focus that the rest, wildly mouthing something at me.

Error code 404

    I become aware how incredibly uncomfortable the recovery position is. I'm finding it hard to hear out of my right ear, being that it's clogged up with shit, piss, and probably man milk for good measure. Therefore, what I don't really need is for someone to have shoved my upturned right hand under my head in such a manner that my knuckles are digging into my left ear like a cork. This is why I can't hear you, you docile twat.

    I suppose the upside of not being able to go and receive emergency medical attention, and thus to miss the opportunity to save my job, is that everybody in uniform is misinterpreting my unwillingness to leave as 'bravery'. I hear an old school screw use the word 'hardcore' which pleases me. The suits also misinterpret my reluctance to leave as 'commitment'. An ambulance has been called for my head wound, which is apparently pretty impressive. A nurse is busy lecturing the Governor next to me about transferable diseases, and how it would be against the prisoner's human rights if the Healthcare Department were to divulge any relevant medical information, held in confidence, about anything that may pose a risk to my health, via the shit-blood mix inside my wound. The Governor agrees by acknowledging that answering a data protection complaint would be complicated, and it is probably best

- in order to avoid litigation - to just assume that I *am* at risk. Just to be on the safe side. I try to interrupt but seemingly my input is distracting from the important legal issue at hand, and thus not required.

I drift over to the shower on the landing and stumble inside. Standing fully uniformed under the dented metallic head, I push the button and lean against the cracked tiles while the piss and shit cocktail is diluted in my hair and washes down my body into the drain. Nobody says anything to me for a few minutes until Gollum appears with a prop bag, which he is waving at me from just outside the steam.

Actual conversation No.15:

Me: Are my eyes blood shot? That looks Red.

Gollum: The uniform stores are empty.

Me: So what have you brought me here, dickhead.

Gollum: A tracksuit.

Me: A tracksuit?

Gollum: Yeah, its a prison tracksuit.

Me: A prisoner's tracksuit?

Gollum: Yeah, it's the best I can do.

Me: You want me to dress like a prisoner, in a prison?

Paul McMahon – Dead Reckoning

Gollum: I don't know what else to…

Me: Fuck off, Gollum.

Gollum: I'm sorry.

Me: Fuck OFF, Gollum

I haven't thought of it before, or if I have I haven't wanted to deal with the finality of clearing it out. I drip all the way down to the 1s to Gav's locker in the staff room. Inside I find a musky shirt and epaulettes and a pair of trousers. I also find a copy of a Howard Marks' *Mr Nice* amongst a load of Kinder egg wrappers, but I have no use for either. I put Gav's clobber on and make my way towards the nurse's hatch on the 1s. Once inside I am seated upon a small stool opposite a poster diagram of a hand, by an enormous Agency nurse who I expect is making more money per hour than I have made so far this shift. She rifles through the unfamiliar drawers looking for something. Lined up on the opposite side of the treatment room there are pots of potions and lotions from the pharmacy delivery that should probably be locked inside the unlocked lockable cabinets above my head. Inside one of these see through bags is a tub of E45 cream.

I am probably not going to be able to last until this afternoon at this rate; my head is killing me, and the Kinder egg up my arse is beginning to feel extremely uncomfortable. My plan to switch the eggs is looking iffy now at best, as I don't know how much of this shift I am going to get through without a drink to numb the pain in my head. Some unknown fucker on the Wing has really taken a serious dislike to me. It must be personal or else Tigger would have put the anchors on it, me being necessary to his business plan and all. There are too many ifs and buts, and I don't like the idea of fingering my arse in a cons cell. It would be so much easier if I could just contaminate the batch I ship in to Tigger, but it's impossible. Tigger's batch has to be clean, so people have to know it comes in clean, so that any contamination is attributable directly to, and only to, Tigger. The blame must be Tigger's alone. I imagine that Tigger, being a professional, has quite an established way of testing the quality, of these things. In my mind, not being an expert in heroin, it would be like trying to sell a bottle of Lambrini to a fine Pinot collector. So I need to switch it when it's safe, when it's seemingly beyond my reach. When it's with the holder. When it's with French.

I can hear the nurse around the corner making vocal sounds into what I presume is a phone or radio, although I have no idea what she is saying. She is trying to dilute her accent down enough so that the words sound a little more like English, but it doesn't sound like she is getting anywhere. I calculate that I have enough time to perform a quick smash and grab on the E45. I'm up and across the medical room like a fat, injured screw, and pierce the bag with my cell key. I pull the tub out and snaffle it away in my fleece, just in time to slam my arse back into the stool unnoticed. The nurse returns with a renewed sense of vigour, targeting a different cupboard, and emerges triumphantly with a bandage. I ask the Nurse for a Terry Butcher, which she doesn't understand so I try for a Stuart Pearce. I'm all for a diverse multicultural society, but I draw the line at my nurses not getting a 'Psycho' reference. In actual fact she hasn't done a bad job; it's not quite as angular as the big man's, but it certainly looks the part.

I make my way to the toilet and sit on the loo with Gav's trousers around my ankles, staring at my index finger. Never again will I be able to eat a Hula Hoop in innocence. Never again will I be at ease wiping sleepy dust out of the corner of my eye. From here on in my relationship with this finger will be strained. I won't ever be able to look at it without being reminded of this - its defining moment.

As soon as I push my finger in my arse, it immediately contracts, making any further advance impossible. Considering we are all on the same team here, my sphincter is acting like a total arsehole. I work my finger up to the distal interphalangeal knuckle joint, around which my sphincter clamps; apparently the name's not down and it's not coming in. The inside of my arse feels like a warm ox's tongue. I can't feel a Kinder egg anywhere and am beginning to wonder how I will explain this in A&E. I reluctantly withdraw my failed finger and change tact. Closing my eyes, I ensure my feet are shoulder-width apart so I have a solid base in readiness to push my stash out. Now there's no longer an intruder to repel, my arse squeezes and my sphincter relaxes in perfect harmony, bringing about the birthing of my Kinder Surprise directly into the water below. It even sounded like a shit, which is lucky as the noise elicits an unexpected laugh from the cubicle next to me. As if this mission wasn't hard enough, I now have to silently fish the shitty egg out with a radio audience. I know which hand is getting it; the right index finger let me down, so is going to be extremely unpopular with his cohorts. I slide in and out like a marine and pocket the egg alongside the E45. The bloke to my left leaves without washing his hands. Upon hearing the door slam, I whip Gav's trousers up and am out the cubicle quicker than you could say "youforgottowipeyourarse". There appears to be no hot water so I start up the hand dryer and hold the E45 underneath to soften the plastic container and seal, all the while watching the door. After a minute I push the hot plastic tub against the side of the sink and pop the malleable lid off. Remembering that French has been dealing this morning, I open the Kinder egg and tap a little of the powder down the sink. I have no real way of knowing how much is left in the real pot but decide that, if anything, there needs to be less in the fake pot than the real one, as somebody else is bound to know where French keeps it, and French may, if anything just blame this hypothetical cheeky mate for helping

Paul McMahon – Dead Reckoning

themselves rather than rightly assume somebody has been up to silly buggers and switched it, like me. I pop the Kinder egg back together and push it down into the cream, using my cell key to shepherd's pie the top, before squeezing theE45 lid back into place.

I convince the S/O to let me finish the session as there is only 30 minutes until lunchtime, and it will do the fuckers' heads in to see me still standing after that. I'm feeling nervous about having a load of heroin in my pocket and just want to get rid of it as soon as possible. The S/O agrees that in the pursuit of team moral it would be good to show resilience and tells me, in that case, to get my arse up to the 3s and get the LBBs done. He tells me if I need him he'll be in his office. Presumably with a bottle.

I impatiently start the daily locks, bolts and bars half way down the landing at French's cell, and tell Oily that it's a method I use to keep the regular 'irregular' and keep the cons on their toes. This he swallows like a goldfish and he darts in first, walloping the window bars with his gigantic palm. I swap the E45 pots with a bit of sleight of hand while Oily is checking the back of the pipes for any new hooch stash. I leave it another three cells before I feign fainting and take Oily's advice.

Actual Conversation No.16:

Oily: Stop being a fucking hero and go home.

Me: Okay, big fella.

My head has stopped hurting, thanks to the drugs flowing round my system; some of them were prescribed. I'm wired to fuck and chewing my face off at the bar after stopping by Gav's to get some 'sleep'. Think about something else. I use the bar payphone to call direct into the wing, telling the desk officer that I had been asked to call in to let them know I am okay. Feeling obliged, he asks if I am okay and I tell him that I'm fine. I leave a pause which he fills straight away with the latest gossip, as predicted. Apparently there has been a massive supply of contaminated heroin flood the wing tonight, and several junkies have been sent to Healthcare and some out to hospital after getting on their cell bells. I can hear the sound of cell doors being kicked and shouts in the background. It sounds as if it is kicking off there tonight. The beautiful thing about this strategy is that it is not just the surviving junkies that will be livid. Every little cog in the whole operation will be livid. The drug 'holders' will be livid, the drug 'runners' will be livid, the 'money men' receiving prison payment will be livid, the 'Baron' will be livid. Those not directly involved but running their own trafficking scams will be livid, as it will bring heat upon the whole Wing. Their equivalents on other Wings will be livid, as it will bring heat on the whole prison. Those outside who arrange the movement of goods and payment will be livid. Their associates will be livid. Those cons inside who are largely unaffected will be livid as everybody else is livid, and it doesn't do you well not to tow the party line. Multiple motives. Motives all focused on Tigger.

I order a celebratory pint and a commemorative chaser, which I down. Out of my change I ask for a second congratulatory pint and a bag of party nuts.

Put ones nose to the grindstone:

I arrive for my late shift with a *very* foggy head. There is a strange atmosphere in the Gate lodge. There are Governors everywhere and a group of police officers are being escorted past me out the gate. I get a little shock when I recognise one of the police officers is Landlubber, here, at my work, with my No.1 Governor. I hope very much his arrival is pure coincidence, and is in no way connected with my not being able to remember whether or not I bumped into any police last night. As I leave the gate and head back into the sterile area I see an Ambulance being escorted into the vehicle lock, and another behind it, waiting. My S/O tells us all to look busy, so unfortunately I really am going to have to 'work' today. Apparently the world and his wife have already been on my Wing already today, and he doesn't want any of us to look as though we don't have anything to do this afternoon. Basically, the briefing is that there have been five junkie deaths overnight, mainly those located in single cells. I'm relieved, therefore, that Landlubber is here on business unrelated to my drunken tomfooleries. None of the bodies were discovered until unlock, when staff were notified by hysterical prisoners who had been unable to rouse two of them. Embarrassingly, two of the remaining three bodies were only discovered at lunchtime when the staff did a controlled feed, letting only a few cells out at a time to collect their lunch. The last body was discovered when the S/O had the bright idea that we should actually check that every prisoner was alive, exactly like we are officially supposed to do in the morning when we relieve the night staff.

In with keeping with the spirit of business I elect to empty the post, which is located outside the hotplate where the prisoners have to pass to collect their food at lunch time, and censor the mail. Not because I'm concerned about maintaining family ties for these scumbags, but because of an ulterior motive. I open the post-box and retrieve the mail. As I had suspected, amongst the envelopes there are two loose pieces of paper with scrawl on them which look like they have been written by a wrong hand. Both of the 'notes' say roughly the same thing.

Paul McMahon – Dead Reckoning

Note No.1:

"The white geezer who shots food on the 3s is gonna die today"

Note No.2

"Get 3-32 off here or he will get mercked up"

I slyly rip both notes into a little pile of confetti and scatter them into the bin under the desk at which at I am sitting. The wing has been searched already, and before long I will be encouraging the Wing Governor, from a decency perspective, to let the prisoners out so they can deal with their grief and seek support from their peers. Think about something else. Sure enough, before long, after much dilly-dallying and deferring of decision-making from Victor 3 to Oscar 1 to the No.1, the decision to open the wing is made and passed down to us to execute. Shit falls downwards.

Poke ones nose in:

Tactically I need to be in situ on the 3s today, in order that I might be able to facilitate a window of opportunity for the assailant(s) to "merk" Tigger. I could leave this in the hitherto lazy hands of my colleagues, who up until now have never been where they are supposed to be, but due to a combination of the S/O's vein trying to escape his neck with stress and there being Governors lurking around, I don't think my colleagues will be their usual useless selves, sitting on their hands doing sweet FA like they normally do. This normally wouldn't be an issue, but for the fact there is a new - and no doubt keen - bloke detailed up there, today of all days. I noticed his name where it shouldn't be this morning. I'm not comfortable with outsiders, but I'm even less comfortable with Tigger having my balls in his hand. Needs must. Therefore, I stage-manage my location as 3s officer by slipping in my two pennies worth in. The S/O is talking to the Governor, who is evidently excited to be near high-ranking police officers as his syllable count is slightly raised. I wait for a suitable moment to butt in, however, as one is not forthcoming I interrupt the Governor whilst he engrossed in a floridly bombastic analysis of the current goings on.

Actual conversation No.17:

Governor: ...a contingency for this precise predicament...

Me: Pardon me Gov, but you need some solid staff on that landing who know the prisoners, to deal with all the shit, Sir.

S/O: Well volunteered, you can baby sit Mr Green.

Microwave Screw

It is obvious that comparisons are going to be unavoidable. It hasn't helped that he is going to be working with me on Gav's and my old landing, that they have given him Gav's vacated locker, Gav's epaulette number, or that his name has taken up the space on the detail where Gav's used to be. So when my S/O warns me that I can't compare this new bloke to Gav, I respectively tell him to fuck off.

Paul McMahon – Dead Reckoning

Mr Green has just been released from Prison Service College at which, he tells me for the second time today, he was awarded the best Officer in section prize. Although his uniform looks identical to mine, as a result of his recent accolade I begin to wander if he is trialling some type of new cutting-edge uniform made of an indestructible fabric - the kind of material that makes a standard stab-proof vest superfluous. I am further convinced of the existence of such a prototype uniform-armour by the manner in which Mr Green is donning it, peacocking down the landing, unlocking doors in front of me as if he has grown a third bollock. I have seen this behaviour before; this is the tell-tale swagger of a man freshly brainwashed by the service into believing that the crown on his cheap nylon epaulette gives him instant protection and immediate Robocop 'Authority'.

'Robocop' Green unlocks 3-32 and a prisoner swiftly exits the cell like a greyhound. Robocop appears to have a short conversation with the remaining occupant which results in the writing of something on his left hand and then the door is locked again, on apparent on request. The remaining occupant is Tigger. Chest forward, Robocop moves off to unlock the rest of the landing without showing much in the way of interest in the decline in association from Tigger. There is a prisoner I don't know the name of smoking on the landing a few doors down from where Robocop has chosen to stand defending his position. Robocop catches a whiff and spins his head round to challenge him. He strides over to the prisoner whilst dipping into a brightly starched breast pocket and pulling out a pristine note pad, ready for action. Robocop informs the prisoner that this is a no smoking establishment, and that smoking is only permitted in his cell. The prisoner looks straight up, momentarily perplexed as he is in the threshold of his cell doorway, then stubs his fag end out on the adjoining cell/landing floor with his trainer. Apparently this is not apologetic enough for Robocop, who demands the prisoner's full name, but the prisoner doesn't look interested in partaking in his own reprimand and averts his gaze to the pool frame being played just beyond Robocop.

Right under one's nose:

Despite the fact the prisoner is standing in his *own* doorway, with a cell card bearing his name *and* prison number right in the foreground of Robocop's gaze, he continues to brandish his shiny new ballpoint and again, much to the amusement of the gathering audience, demands the prisoners name.

I decide to let this one play itself out without any meddling from me. Robocop will thank me for it later I'm sure, having had the chance to set his stall out and prove himself no lemon. Think about something else.

The prisoner tells Robocop that his name is Head. Richard Head. Robocop appears to write down the name in full and, smiling inanely like an Indian with his first scalp, informs the prisoner that he will be issuing an IEP warning, and that he must not be caught doing this again or there will be hell to pay. I am not really sure what hell he imagines paying him, through the puny force of the prison services discipline procedures. Anyhow, the prisoner doesn't appear to be listening, distracted by something amusing that Robocop can't quite place. Oblivious, Robocop turns and saunters back toward where I am standing, almost out of earshot from the chuckles.

I decide that this is definitely the right time to give Robocop the benefit of my experience.

Paul McMahon – Dead Reckoning

Actual conversation No.18:

Me: Now listen, er..?

Robocop: Jeff...

Me: Jeff, listen Jeff...

Jeff: ...Mr Green, sorry, It's Mr Green when we're on the landing though, as there's prisoners...

Me: Look, shut up a second, will ya? You seem like a decent bloke, so I'm going to tell you a few things that you need to listen to, right?

Mr Green: Er...Yeah alright.

Me: You need to forget everything you got taught at college, right...

Mr Green: (Laughs)

Me: What's funny?

Mr Green: Sorry, it's just they said we would get told that.

Me: Who?

Mr Green: Our tutor at college, they said that we would come to our establishments and we would get told that by the older staff.

Me: Right, and why?

Mr Green: They said that we would be coming in and doing things properly, upsetting the apple cart.

Paul McMahon – Dead Reckoning

Me: Properly? Really? What else did they say? Did they tell you to wear your tie, even though it's the middle of the fucking summer?

Mr Green: Well…It's professional.

Me: The Governor says we can take them off in the summer.

Mr Green: We should continue to set examples to the residents…

Me: …not residents, cons. We don't work in a fucking old people's home.

Mr Green: Well offenders then. The tie is a metaphor for the pro-social modelling approach.

Me: What??

Mr Green: It's like - if they see us behave in a certain way, then they will aspire to…

Me: To? Give up being a wrong'un on the out, because you wore your tie in July?

Mr Green: Well no obviously not, but it's part of a holistic approach to encourage the desistance of crime.

Me: Holistic? Desistance? Fuck me…what a cunt.

To put ones nose out of joint:

      Our first shift together is not going as I hoped. I rant at Robocop that when I joined the job nobody would speak to you unless you had five years in, that I was making tea for the dinosaurs

Paul McMahon – Dead Reckoning

until some other sprog joined up for me to ignore, and I express my dissatisfaction at being confronted by an arrogant prick, who's got less time in than I have had on the sick, telling me to wear my fucking tie. This has definitely taken the wind out of his sails. From this distance I can now see that our uniforms are identical, aside from the fact that my shirt is an interesting shade of off-ivory and his is as white as the northern star.

Mr Green nervously pushes his glasses back up his sweaty nose and I can see the pen jotting on his left hand reads "3-32 S/O". I seize upon this immediately, explaining to the sprog that the S/O is there for us, not the prisoners. That the S/O does not, and should not, be getting involved in running the landing. I try and appeal to Robocop's sense of self-importance by explaining that the prisoner is just trying to navigate round him, go above his head and mug him off. This appears to strike a chord with Robocop. So much so that he spits on his hand and rubs it off. Narcissistic personality disorder? Bingo.

Seeing that I have knocked him down a peg or two, and recognising that I ought now to bring him up a little, I tell Mr Green that he is our landing's alarm bell response and that if there is an alarm bell anywhere in the prison that he must attend the scene. He seems pleased with this and claps his palms together in anticipation. Being that I need rid of him to deal with Tigger, he won't have to wait long. I begin to scan the environment for plausible reasons to dispatch Mr Green off on some task or another. I will have to be clever about this one, as yesterday somebody from Reception sent him to the stores asking for some X-Rays for the X-Ray machine. Out the window, at the end of the landing down to our exercise yard, I can see a group of prisoners being escorted on a short cut from C-Wing First Night Centre to G-Wing by a member of staff and I have a flash of inspiration.

Paul McMahon – Dead Reckoning

To 'swing the lamp':

One of the cons crossing the yard is covered in tattoos and has a shaved head. He begins to shout up to the windows in search of someone called Buggsy, who after two or three shouts, answers, calling out the shaved fella's name "Stevo". Perfect. I jump on the phone and contact G-Wing, to enquire which landing Officer 'A-to-Z' is on. A-to-Z's actual name contains almost all the letters of the alphabet, and in a hurry A-to-Z is much easier to say than Olatundifagbenle. In an emergency every syllable counts. After redialling on the appropriate number I get through to A-to-Z . After exchanging a few good humoured insults I cut to the chase and let him know about the fella I have just "heard" on the yard talking about the "... big black Nigger" who banged him up last time on G-Wing who is going to "...get what's coming to him". A flap of a butterfly's wing. Think about something else. A-to-Z thanks me for the heads up and assures me that he will be having a little career chat with 'Nazi Stevo' when he gets up to his landing, upon which there were no spaces until this phone rang. He will make a space for his little friend. A-to-Z tells me that he owes me one, and that he will shout me a pint next time he sees me down the 'Prince' Pub. Result.

It has been about five minutes since I called A-to-Z and I have calculated that 'Nazi Stevo' will have been received, processed, allocated a cell, and should be about to meet his maker. So confident am I that there will be a bell that I can't resist the opportunity to show off a little jail craft sixth sense; that, and earn a little drinking money for tonight. In the spirit of comradery, I suggest a little bet with Robocop that there will be an alarm bell within the next five minutes. Robocop is all too willing to take up the bet as he evidently can't wait to get stuck in to some 'real action'. As we are shaking hands the warble on both our radios go off. Robocop's eyes widen, and he tries to run off in every direction at once. I tighten my grip, and suggest double or nothing, nominating G-Wing as my location. Robocop nods, trying to pull

Paul McMahon – Dead Reckoning

his hand away to run even though he still doesn't know what direction he should be going. The call quickly comes over the net, "Alarm Bell G-Wing". Robocop slides his sweaty hand out, exclaiming his disbelief with a simple "FUCK" and sprints off down the landing toward the stairs. A tenner should take the edge off after work.

To out Herod, Herod:

No sooner than Robocop has left the landing, I'm walking toward 3-32 with my keys gripped in my sweaty palm. I open the door without looking through the observation panel as I don't want to lose my nerve, and shoot the bolt in one swift movement so Tigger can't shut the door. I carry on walking, fixing my gaze on the staircase I intend to climb away from any involvement in what I am sure is about to happen. The last cell next to the stairs is blaring hip hop extremely loudly. I push open the door on the way past, allowing the sound of 'Nigga's' and 'gunshots' to flood the landing in volume, and make my getaway fast, Tupac drive-by style. I don't hear much in the way of noise upstairs. There is a lot going on. Alarm bell situations are stressful for everybody, so I can't really be expected to be everywhere at the same time, especially as my 'oppo' has responded to an alarm bell which he shouldn't have done. Somebody should have a word with him. After all, I'm just one man in a crazy world trying to make a difference. Think about something else.

The Mary Celeste:

On my return to the 3s there is a palpable sense of tension. Prisoners aren't going about their usual business. Cell doors are pushed to, and the pool equipment lies still on the table. The pin phones are swinging like they have been dropped in mid-use. Further down the landing there are one or two men standing in cell doorways peering out, their collective focus on me. When I turn to meet their gaze they avert their eyes and disappear back into their cells. Everybody is waiting for me to find something. I saunter as innocently as I'm able down the landing, looking in every cell as routinely as I can replicate until I reach 3-32.

Moment of Reckoning:

I didn't know how much blood the body is capable of holding, but if this were a pub quiz I would have been way off the mark. Tigger is lying in an enormous pool of it, motionless. If this had been a film set, and I the Director, I would have fired the effects team immediately for visual melodrama. Claret is everywhere, on the walls and on the ceiling. What is left of his t-shirt has ridden up his midriff, exposing a wodge of magazines that have been wedged down his jeans, under his belt, so they poke up over his lower torso in what can only be some kind of improvised stab vest. Clever? Yes, but ultimately futile. He is holding in his dead hand a rather impressive blade, fashioned out of a metal chair bracket, straightened and sharpened; the handle part looks to be wrapped in some kind of ripped prison jean segment. You can't actually place a corpse on report for damaging prison property, even though they are officially still on the prison numbers, but I would if I could, such is my hatred for this ex-fucker. The blade itself is clean and obviously unused. He evidently didn't even get a chance. Upon closer inspection of Tigger's carcass it is clear why the blade, it being a close quarters weapon remains unused, as the weapon that snuffed out Tigger was most definitely not a hand-to-hand combat weapon, but more of a 'pull the trigger' sort of a weapon. It occurs to me that hip hop was a good choice of cover

Paul McMahon – Dead Reckoning

music as the pop of this pistol would have slipped into the collective sounds of the landing incognito.

To my utter relief I see a pistol lying on the floor of the cell next to Tigger's body. My spring must be in this pistol. Just to be on the safe side, I pick it up with a freshly gloved hand and drop it into the cell kettle, before flicking the switch. DNA and water don't see eye to eye. I watch CSI. The kettle boils immediately. Tigger was caught mid-brew it seems. I pluck the pistol out of the water and drop it into an empty latex glove to 'preserve the evidence'. Not having a proper evidence box at hand, and knowing I am not supposed to let go of it now until some fancy chap from the Met turns up to take possession of it, I put it in my fleece pocket and do the zip right up. For security.

S.O.S:

I get on the radio and report an "URGENT MESSAGE" using correct radio procedure to the Emergency Control Room. The radio operator in the control room berates me for using the word "MESSAGE", and goes into a monologue that I can't interrupt on the radio until she finishes sending, that the word M*****E is *only* to be used when there is an emergency and not for general communication, as per the Prison Service Order. When she has finished I put through the URGENT MESSAGE again. This time she asks me to stand down as she is talking to a member of the works party who need to escort a contractor with a ladder into the boiler room. While I am waiting for this exchange to finish I take a seat on the pool table. When this has finished I try a third time. This time she asks me if this is a training exercise, which I assure her it is not. Only after warning me that if this is a joke she will be taking this up with her manager does she, several minutes later, actually sound a general alarm and put out a call for Victor 3 to attend the Wing. Immediately.

Paul McMahon – Dead Reckoning

With nothing else to do, and conscious of the fact that the bones of this incident will be dug over many times from all sorts of managerial grades, I decide to try and act in a manner that is indisputably professional, and imagine what I would do in this situation if I actually cared. I opt for securing the landing, which is pretty default really for any incident. I go round and start to bang up the doors of the cells nearest to me, ushering prisoners into their cells. This is incredibly easy as they are all stood off the landing in their doorways already. I can now hear a herd of officers stampeding up the stairs onto my landing behind me, and suddenly remember that I've seen a dead body. The thought occurs to me that I should feign shock, for use by a defence barrister in any future court case, but I don't know whether it would look weird as my colleagues would probably think I was taking the piss.

I point at 3-32 and let the onrushing Oscar 1 know that there is one 'brown bread' in there. A moment later, once he has jolted off towards the cell, I also quickly shout out for him NOT to open the door so as to MAINTAIN THE INTEGRITY OF THE CRIME SCENE. My barrister would have a field day with that. What conspirator to murder would want to maintain the integrity of the crime scene for the collection of scientific evidence that may have them convicted? None. This is going rather well. I shout all this out as I know full well that screws being screws will want to have a look. The urge to have a goosy gander outweighs our scenes of crime training every time. That door is getting opened whether I like it or not. That door *is* opened, as luck would have it, by Victor 3 who has muscle-ranked Oscar 1 out of the way. Victor 3 lets out a noise like an orgasm, and the marauding crowd behind him pushes forward, sending him directly into the cell whereupon he slips up in the claret. As he falls over he grabs hold of the nearest thing to him, which happens to be Oscar 1 who goes down with him in apparent solidarity. The sound of the kerfuffle encourages yet more uniformed bodies into the cell, not knowing if there is a scuffle they should be getting involved in, meaning that there is a bit of a Hillsborough happening at the front. There is now more DNA in that cell than at a bukkake party. I feel acquitted already.

A shoulder to cry on:

I am sitting with the 'Care Team'. When they say 'Care' they mean 'incapable', and when they say 'Team' they mean 'Gollum'. The 'Care Team' course is the only one that Gollum could get on; the Control and Restraint boys didn't want him, nor did the Hostage lads, even the Self-harm division didn't want him dragging them down - so he has ended up on the 'Care Team'. It appears that I have to see 'Incapable Gollum' so that the Prison can tick the employee support box. It is rather awkward. We have been sitting in silence for about two minutes; I am not emoting for this fucker for all the coke in Bolivia. I don't know what to say to him anyway. After I can bear his hand wrangling no more, I ask him if *he* is ok. He says that he feels a bit nervous as he has never done this before. I assure him that it will be okay. There is a another excruciating pause that is interrupted by the sound of a droplet of something moist landing on the desk over which Gollum is leaning toward me. It can only have originated from somewhere around where his anxious expression is pulsating at me. Although I am thankful for this distraction from the unbearable stillness, I don't wait long enough to establish whether this is a sweat-based interruption or a tear based interruption. Having had quite enough 'counselling', bid him farewell and prepare to make a hurried exit starboard.

It dawns on me as I stand to leave that I should have made the Duty Governor aware of the presence of a gun in one of Her Majesty's Prisons as soon as was reasonably possible. What with all the fuss over the body I've clean forgotten about it until I've put my hand in my fleece pocket instead of shaking Gollum's outstretched hand. I have a wicked urge to shoot Gollum here and

Paul McMahon – Dead Reckoning

now, and claim PTSD. It is a good enough a defence for Frankland prisoners who try and murder staff, so I might get away with it - Gollum did try to dress me up like a Con, and everybody knows how much stress I've been under. After indulging in the fantasy for a few seconds, I ask Gollum to call the ECR and ask them to arrange for a firearms officer from the Met to come and take possession of the gun. Every Tom, Dick and Harry wants to try a 'Clint Eastwood' with it but I decline, quoting about continuity of evidence. The No.1 Governor would love it.

Spread-Eagle Oratory:

The No.1 Governor does love it. His syllable count goes through the roof. Evidently, I am as brave as I am honorificabilitudinitatibus. Now I don't like sesquipedalian hyperbole as a rule, but I think I'm being complimented so I am going to let it go this once.

I am told that what I have been through is 'horrendous', that I have done more than expected of me in the line of duty, especially with my gallantry in the hostage situation the other day, which he decides to belatedly bring up now. I am told that the prisoner is now back in the community and that he owes his liberty to me, so serious could have been the charges had the incident got out of control. The lateness of this praise has somewhat diluted my enjoyment of it. I am further told that my discovery of a firearm in his jail has prevented a potential escape in which staff could realistically have been killed, which would in turn have caused the Governor to fail two of his Key Performance Indicators. I'm told that in light of this, I may have a move of my choice, anywhere in the system, as a thank you if I should so wish one. Seemingly, in my case, the gratitude of the service knows no bounds. Apparently this is an 'unequivocal guarantee without caveat'. The Governor imparts to me that he is related, through marriage, to the Area Manager, who is a personal friend of the Prisons Minister and an occasional mover and shaker in the same Bridge League as the Justice Secretary. The beautiful thing about being part of the Commonwealth is that there are far-lung reaches of the 'Empire' that still need to bang people up British-style, and so one exists like a little HMP enclave in foreign shores. So I ask for it; to test the water. As it turns out, the Service's gratitude does have its limits, and I have asked for the one thing that is 'understandably' out of the question, due to relocation costs, etc. The Governor does not actually say 'no', he merely points out the excellent opportunities that the English prison system allegedly has to offer. I decline a move, as I know these waters comfortingly well.

I'm coming to terms with being a murderer, of sorts. I expected more inner turmoil. Truth be told, it doesn't feel any different than before Tigger's moment of reckoning. Officially, I have not encouraged others to kill or engaged in the planning of the event with any of those responsible. I think it would be hard to pin any sort of conspiracy charge on me. In fact, I genuinely don't know who did it although, if I was a betting man I would have to say French. I am a betting man, in fact, and I *have* backed French in the book that Oily is running. I'll have to find out through word of mouth though, as I have been given 'gardening leave'. To keep in with the spirit of the gesture, I set off for the 'Anchor in Hope' pub to spend today in a beer garden, seeing as though I don't actually have a garden of my own to spend it in.

After getting a pint of ale from the bar, I take the fire exit out into the beer garden and select the most comfortable looking of the well-built wooden garden chairs to soak up the brilliant sunshine. I am about to get hammered in the Governor's time; a pint doesn't taste much better than this. Dreamily I fold a paper lunch menu into a boat. I use no devices or tools, but absentmindedly judge the angles using the edge of the table as a 'north star' by which to plot each crease and fold. I am in no way accomplished in the art of origami but this vessel is a beauty. It is symmetrical, which pleases me, as nothing else about me is so ordered. I am serenely happy with my creation. Its sail is dead-centre and its hull unfolds at port and starboard equally in height and depth. I place the boat upon the table at which I'm sitting and move my pint towards the back of the table, so as not to crowd her, spilling a little and christening her in ale. As I do so I glimpse in my peripheral vision and in the reflection on my beer glass, a shape, whilst a simultaneous shadow is cast over the table, changing the conditions for sailing. Then comes a sound, like a clap of thunder.

Weigh Anchor

My boat looks even better from this angle, with my head slumped on top of the table. My left ear is pressed against the shining varnished tabletop, which looks to me in this moment like a windless, still sea surface extending out into the horizon of my vision. I have no idea who delivered the blow. The list is endless. The annual turnover of prisoners at work is massive, and those I have turned over out of work are fair in number also. This is overdue. I'm unable to move, or feel, anything. Due to the force of the blow, my hearing is dulled as though I'm underwater. I am powerless to avert my gaze from my beautiful boat.

Hoist the Blue Peter:

In the foreground of my vision I see a dark, red stream flow out from underneath my head, surging slowly toward my boat. I feel misty. The stream turns into a river and pushes forward in slow-motion, flowing under the hull of my boat and rising her up fluidly forward on her voyage out to sea. I am drifted.

Paul McMahon – Dead Reckoning

If there is one water in Europe I want, it is the black
cold pool where into the scented twilight
a child squatting full of sadness launches
a boat as fragile as a butterfly in May.

I can no more, bathed in your langours, O waves,
sail in the wake of the carriers of cottons;
nor undergo the pride of the flags and pennants;
nor pull past the horrible eyes of prison hulks.

Arthur Rimbaud 1871

The Drunken Boat

Printed in Great Britain
by Amazon